Crack!

Someone was shooting at them!

Liam hit the gas and Shauna braced herself for the worst. Her body began to shake uncontrollably as the SUV sped up and jerked from side to side as Liam attempted to escape.

They were shooting at her this time, not just attempting to run her off the road.

These people, whoever they were, wanted her dead.

Just like her mother.

Why? She couldn't seem to grasp why she'd suddenly become a target. It just didn't make any sense. Tears pricked her eyes, but she held them back.

"Are you okay?" Liam asked tersely.

She hesitantly lifted her head. "I— Yes."

"I wish I knew exactly where the gunfire came from." He sounded frustrated. "This is my fault. I knew you were in danger, but I didn't expect anyone to fire at us in broad daylight."

"At *me*." Her voice was soft, but firm. "Not you, Liam. This is all about me."

Laura Scott has always loved romance and read faith-based books by Grace Livingston Hill in her teenage years. She's thrilled to have been given the opportunity to retire from thirty-eight years of nursing to become a full-time author. Laura has published over thirty books for Love Inspired Suspense. She has two adult children and lives in Milwaukee, Wisconsin, with her husband of thirty-five years. Please visit Laura at laurascottbooks.com, as she loves to hear from her readers.

Books by Laura Scott

Love Inspired Suspense

Hiding in Plain Sight

Justice Seekers

Soldier's Christmas Secrets
Guarded by the Soldier
Wyoming Mountain Escape
Hiding His Holiday Witness
Rocky Mountain Standoff
Fugitive Hunt

Rocky Mountain K-9 Unit

Hiding in Montana

Visit the Author Profile page at LoveInspired.com for more titles.

HIDING IN PLAIN SIGHT

LAURA SCOTT

LOVE INSPIRED SUSPENSE
INSPIRATIONAL ROMANCE

LOVE INSPIRED® SUSPENSE

INSPIRATIONAL ROMANCE

Recycling programs
for this product may
not exist in your area.

ISBN-13: 978-1-335-58721-3

Hiding in Plain Sight

Love Inspired
22 Adelaide St. West, 41st Floor
Toronto, Ontario M5H 4E3, Canada
www.LoveInspired.com

Printed in U.S.A.

I sought the Lord and he heard me,
and delivered me from all my fears.
—*Psalm* 34:4

This book is dedicated to Sally Nowak,
who has been waiting for this book for a long time!

ONE

Shauna McKay's cell phone rang as she followed her classmates into the chilly, dark Illinois fall night. Their business law midterm exam had been tough, but she felt good about it. Now they had a full week off until classes started up again.

Her phone continued ringing, so she dug around in her backpack for the device. When she noticed her mother's name on the screen, she grimaced.

"Hi, Mom. What's up? I don't have a lot of time. I'm just leaving campus now and need to go straight to work."

"Shauna, listen carefully." Her mother's whispered tone screamed urgency. "I need you to leave Chicago right now. Don't go to work—they'll find you there."

"Who will find me? What are you talking about?" Shauna's patience with her mother's issues was wearing thin. For the past few weeks, her mother had claimed she'd noticed people following her. Coming after her. Her mom might be off booze and drugs, but the synapses in her brain cells still didn't work as well as they should. This call was likely yet another example of her mom's worsening paranoia.

"This is serious. I'm being followed. Go to Green Lake to find your uncle David. He'll keep you safe."

A shiver of apprehension slunk down her spine. The panicked desperation in her mom's voice was new. And her mom had never told her to go find Uncle Davy before. "Mom, maybe we should get together. I'll call in sick to work. Where are you?"

"No! Don't come here. *Find David!*"

Before Shauna could say anything more, there was a muffled thud, then a startled cry before the line went dead.

"Mom? Mom!" Shauna pushed the redial button, but the call went straight to voice mail.

"What's wrong?" asked her classmate Jeff Clancy. He was already going bald at thirty-three and was ten years her senior and a great study partner. Thankfully, he was also one of the few men who didn't seem to want anything from her other than friendship. Which was all she had to give.

"I don't know." She desperately hit Redial again and again, but each time without success. Shauna felt sick to her stomach. Something was wrong. Very wrong. "I have to head home to check on my mom."

"I'll come with you."

Shauna nodded, grateful she wouldn't have to go alone. Her mom hadn't asked her to call the police, and while she knew that was the logical next step, she couldn't quite bring herself to do it.

Her mother and the police didn't exactly get along. Too much history. Too many prior arrests.

"Hurry," she said, abruptly sprinting toward her car, her backpack bouncing against her side.

Jeff tried to keep up, his wheezing breaths proving that he didn't do any type of running on a regular basis. Not that she was a track star.

Jamming the key into the ignition, she fired up the engine while Jeff scrambled to buckle his seat belt. She took off, tires squealing as she headed toward the highway. The Carlisle Chicago Community College campus wasn't too far from the Hidden Pines trailer park that her mother called home.

The headlights from her car slashed through the darkness as she turned onto Hidden Pines Road, illuminating the dilapidated and poverty-stricken trailers that were parked far too close together for comfort or privacy. The name of the park was due to a whopping six pine trees scattered among the cramped community, one right next to her mother's place.

When she pulled up in front of her mother's trailer, most of the windows were dark, except for the light that her mom normally left on above the kitchen sink. Was her mom even home? Or had she called Shauna from somewhere else?

No! Don't come here, her mom had said. Shauna figured for sure that meant her mother was at home.

Her mom didn't drive—too many DUIs and no cash to purchase a car even if she wanted to—so the absence of a vehicle in the driveway didn't mean anything. Yet Shauna couldn't seem to shake the impending sense of doom that cloaked her as she threw the gearshift into Park and cut the engine.

"Shauna, wait! Maybe you shouldn't—" Jeff protested.

She shot out of the car and slammed the driver's-side door, cutting him off. Jeff could follow or not, his choice.

"Mom?" Shauna found the screen door unlocked and ignored her deepening panic. "Mom! Are you okay?"

Dark mahogany stains on the yellowed linoleum floor of the narrow hallway caused her to stop in her tracks. Was that blood?

"No, please, no…" She forced herself to move forward, one step, then another.

Until she could see her mother's body lying on the kitchen floor, sticky with blood.

"Mom!" She rushed forward, hoping she wasn't too late.

No pulse. Cool skin. Too much blood. And, worst of all, a large butcher knife embedded in her mom's chest.

Shauna didn't realize she was sobbing until Jeff pulled her away from her mother's dead body. He gave her a hard shake.

"Shauna, snap out of it. You need to stay back. This is a crime scene. We have to call the police."

She lurched sideways, shrinking from Jeff's touch. Her mind could barely comprehend what had happened. In the depths of her mind, she realized Jeff was right. This was a crime scene.

Her mother had been brutally murdered.

She turned and staggered into the tiny bathroom, losing the contents of her stomach in one sickening lurch. Tears filled her eyes, but even through her blurred vision she could see that her hands and clothes were stained with her mother's blood.

What had happened here? Why had her mother been murdered?

On the other side of the bathroom door, Shauna heard Jeff speaking to the 911 operator. She quickly washed off as much of the blood as possible, then abruptly exited the bathroom, brushing past him to head outside.

The cool October breeze didn't help clear her head. She could still see the horrific knife. Smell the metallic scent of blood. Feel the icy coldness of her mother's skin.

Without stopping to think it through, she jumped behind the wheel of her white Honda Civic and cranked the key. From the doorway of her mother's trailer, Jeff shouted at her to stop, to wait, but she jerked the gearshift into Reverse, backed up, then cranked the wheel and drove away.

Jeff could wait there to talk to the police, but she wasn't going to. She didn't trust the cops.

Especially when it came to anything related to her mom.

Tears streamed down her face, blurring her vision. She swiped at her eyes, and then grabbed her mobile phone from the cup holder where she'd dropped it earlier.

Unfortunately, her attempt to call her uncle didn't go through. A mechanical voice informed her that her uncle's phone was no longer in service.

Her stomach clenched painfully. Was Davy hurt, too? Was someone murdering her entire family?

Gripping the steering wheel tightly, Shauna headed for the interstate. She'd been to her uncle Davy's place, located in a rural area of Green Lake, before. Granted, that was just over two years ago, but she hoped she'd still remember where it was.

And that she wouldn't find her uncle dead. Like her mom.

If her mother's panicked claims held any kernel of truth, Shauna was next.

Shauna stopped for gas several times, using up her meager supply of cash. She was afraid to use her credit or debit cards. No sense in leaving an electronic trail for either the police or the murderer to follow.

The idea that someone had killed her mother and was now after her, as well, was incomprehensible. After the initial shock had faded, her mind whirled with questions. She didn't understand why on earth either one of them would be a target. Granted, her mother might have made a few enemies along the way—mostly low-level drug dealers—but her mom had been clean for the past few years. So why would one of them come after her now? None of it made any sense.

Yet the memory of her mother's bloodstained trailer proved the magnitude of danger.

Guilt hit hard. She'd often been impatient with her mother, had gotten irritated with her mother's neediness.

Now her mother was gone for good.

I'm sorry, Mom. So sorry I didn't believe you.

Tears threatened again, so she swiped her face and focused on the road. The recent dusting of October snow made for a few slippery spots. She desperately wished she could talk to Davy. Why wasn't his phone in service? Because he'd stopped paying his bills? *Wait a minute.* She frowned. Where was her mom's phone? The attack had happened mere seconds before their call had been disconnected. Shauna had heard her mom's startled cry. If she'd dropped the phone, it would have been lying somewhere nearby.

She racked her brain, thinking back to the grotesque crime scene. Her mother's phone hadn't been anywhere in sight. At least, not on the floor beside her, the way she'd expect it would be if her mother had been interrupted by the attacker.

So where was it? Had the murderer taken it? And if so, why?

Her gaze dropped to her mobile phone sitting in the cup holder beside her. A shiver rippled through her body, and she instinctively shrank from the device, as if it were a copperhead snake that might strike out and bite with razor-sharp fangs.

The murderer could very well have taken her mom's phone to get Shauna's number.

Now who was being paranoid? She struggled to take several deep breaths. Why hadn't she taken her mom's fears more seriously? If she had listened, her mother would still be alive.

She lowered the window and tossed the phone out, listening as it shattered on the hard pavement. No point in keeping it, since she didn't have anyone else to call.

There wasn't a lot of traffic on the road. As time passed, she eventually grew closer to Madison, Wisconsin. She winced when a blinding pair of twin headlights hit her eyes, reflecting off the rearview mirror.

At first she was simply annoyed, but then the high beams grew closer. Zooming up until the vehicle was right behind her.

Too close.

Shauna instinctively braced herself, even as she tried to increase her speed.

No! She saw it happen as if in slow motion. The vehicle slammed into her, causing her to lose control of her small car. She gasped when the car slid into the side rail. The impact of the blow caused the airbags to deploy, punching her in the face with enough force to make her cry out in pain.

And there was nothing but air as her car flipped, falling over the side of the road and down to the snow-dusted wooded area below.

Green Lake County sheriff Liam Harland took the circular entrance ramp onto the highway, heading due north, grateful to leave the state capital behind. Visiting the cemetery where his wife and son were buried only reminded him of his colossal failures. Guilt stretched like a heavy yoke across his shoulders, chaining him forever to the mistakes of his past.

He'd barely cleared the interchange when he heard the high-pitched screech of metal crashing against metal. When he glanced in his rearview mirror, he saw something white falling through the air and landing in a mass of trees below.

Was that a car?

There was a jagged break in the side rail of the highway ramp, proving he hadn't imagined the incident. Reacting instinctively, Liam yanked the steering wheel hard to the right, pulling off on the shoulder of the interstate and punching the brakes to bring his SUV to an abrupt stop. Grabbing his phone, he dialed 911 and reported the accident. After providing his information,

Liam tucked the phone in the pocket of his denim jacket and dodged through traffic to get closer to the scene.

He could see what looked to be a small white vehicle lying upside down, suspended within the tree branches. The windows were shattered, likely from when the airbags had deployed. For a split second he saw a different vehicle—one lying in a ditch, a navy blue four-door, the roof crushed in on the occupants inside. He blinked the two-year-old image away, returning to reality with a jarring thud.

Without the slightest hesitation, Liam made his way down the edge of the ravine. Maybe there wasn't anything he could do to help, but he needed to try. He was halfway to the bottom when he heard a woman cry out as the car slid from its perch, crashing to the ground below.

No! Liam covered the distance as quickly as possible, his heart thundering in his chest by the time he reached the vehicle. The first thing he noticed was a flash of pale skin streaked with blood through the driver's-side window.

"Are you okay?" he shouted, pushing through the brush to reach the door. "Help is on the way."

"I'm—all right," a female voice said.

Liam hunkered down near the car, trying to peer inside. "Don't move around too much," he cautioned. "The paramedics will be here soon to check you out. You might have hidden spinal cord injuries."

"Hanging upside down is making me feel sick. Please help me get out of here before I throw up."

The night was still and silent—no wail of sirens indicating help was imminent. Liam tugged on the driver's-side door and amazingly was able to pry it open enough to reach inside.

"Hold still," he warned, rocking back on his heels and pulling his penknife from the front pocket of his jeans. "I'm going to cut the belt, okay?"

"Thank you." Her voice was barely above a whisper, and her face was veiled with a curtain of dark hair. Her hands were pressed against the steering wheel. She wasn't tall enough to reach the roof of the car below her, and he understood her discomfort when he noticed her legs were braced on the sides, as if to help ease the pressure from being held up by the seat belt.

Bits of shattered glass littered the area as he went to work on the seat belt. Sawing through the thick fabric of the belt was more difficult than he'd anticipated. He used his shoulder and back as a brace to prop the woman up so that she wouldn't fall once he'd gotten rid of the restraint. When the edges of the belt finally separated, she sagged against him. Liam made sure to tuck the knife out of the way before gently assisting the woman down and away from the vehicle.

She leaned against him for a moment, surrounding him with an evergreen scent, before moving away.

"What's your name?" he asked.

"Shauna."

He waited for a last name, but none was forthcoming. Maybe her head injury was worse than he'd thought. "Are you sure you're okay?"

"Yes." She crawled over to sit against the closest tree trunk. She tipped her head back and relaxed against the rough bark, as if grateful to be in a normal position again.

She looked younger than he'd expected, for some

reason. Feeling ancient at twenty-eight, Liam turned his attention to what was left of the damaged car.

One thing for certain—it was totaled.

The shrill of sirens filled the night, and Liam couldn't help feeling relieved that the paramedics would be here any minute. There wasn't a lot of blood, and quite honestly, he'd expected more based on the way the car had gone over the edge of the overpass. Shauna had sustained a cut to her forehead, and he was surprised that the laceration was already clotted over. Most head wounds bled a lot. But other than the cut, he didn't see any obvious signs of injuries.

However, internal damage was more likely to kill a victim of blunt trauma. At least, that was what he'd been told after losing Jerica and Mikey.

"Thanks for getting me out," Shauna said, breaking into his thoughts.

"What happened?" Liam asked, going into cop mode. This wasn't his jurisdiction, and dressed as he was in blue jeans and a quilted jacket, it wasn't likely she knew he had a background in law enforcement.

"I—uh, went too fast and lost control." The pause made it sound as if she were lying. "The accident is entirely my fault."

"Frankly, I'm surprised you're alive," Liam said in a brusque tone. He had no idea why she'd survived when his wife and infant son hadn't.

"Would you mind grabbing my backpack?"

Liam obliged, heading over to peer into the car. He found the pack, which didn't look bad, considering how it must have been tossed around, and carried it over to set it at her side.

"Thank you," she murmured.

An ambulance and two squad cars arrived, parking on the shoulder where he'd left his vehicle. He glanced up again at the crushed safety railing, thinking that it should have kept the car from going over if the driver had simply lost control from taking the ramp too fast. Unless she'd been speeding? He moved around to the back of the car, taking in the severely dented rear bumper. Using his flashlight app, he tried to decipher if the dents were fresh or rusty from a crash that had happened long ago.

Not his crime scene, he reminded himself as he pocketed his phone and returned to where Shauna was seated. This was the jurisdiction of the Dane County Sheriff's Department, who'd just arrived.

It didn't take long for the two deputies to escort the paramedic teams down the steep sides of the ravine. As they moved closer, Liam grimaced when he recognized Deputy Jason O'Connor, the same cop who'd found his wife and son that fateful night two years ago when Jerica had accidentally crashed their car into a tree, killing herself and their son on impact.

Yeah, talk about a coincidence.

"Well, if it isn't Liam Harland," Deputy O'Connor drawled, aiming the beam of flashlight dead center on Liam's face, making him lift his hand to block the offending glare. "What are *you* doing here so far from home?"

O'Connor's sneer wasn't very subtle, but Liam kept his tone neutral, refusing to rise to the bait. For some unknown reason, the deputy had taken a strong dislike to Liam. Maybe because Liam was in a position of higher authority. Whatever, it didn't matter. Deep down, he knew he deserved contempt. If not for his personal failures, the inability to make his wife happy, maybe she and their son would still be alive.

He shoved those useless thoughts aside. "Saw the car go over the railing, called 911 and then came down to make sure the occupant was okay."

The deputy's flashlight swept the area, zeroing in on the upside-down car and then finding the driver who'd managed to escape seemingly unscathed. Liam wasn't impressed when O'Connor and his partner didn't bother to look up at the bent and broken railing lining the overpass, which, in his opinion, was the real scene of the crime.

Not his case. Not his problem.

From the corner of his eye, Liam narrowed his gaze when he noticed that Shauna's demeanor changed dramatically, from the gratefulness she'd shown him to a wary suspicion at the arrival of the authorities.

His instincts screamed that something was off about this scenario. In his experience, innocent people trusted the police to help them when they were in trouble. They were up-front and honest about what had transpired, especially in a near-fatal collision. He moved to the side, checking out the mashed back bumper of the car once again.

No, the details didn't add up, which meant Shauna had been less than forthright about the event. He was convinced she was hiding something. But what?

And, even more important, why?

TWO

Shauna had loathed every minute of being questioned by Dane County deputy sheriff O'Connor. She doubted he had believed her version of events, especially when he'd insisted on doing drug and alcohol testing. The deputy had looked surprised that her results had been clean.

Her head ached, the cut above her right eyebrow requiring a few stitches. Sitting in the emergency department of the Madison hospital, she had no idea how she'd get to Green Lake. The city was almost two hours away. Yet, as she was being discharged from the hospital, her rescuer, Liam Harland, had shown up, offering a ride.

Sheriff Harland, she mentally corrected. O'Connor had mentioned during their interview that Liam was the Green Lake County sheriff.

After the way she'd been rammed off the road, nearly to her death, she'd been hesitant to accept Liam's kind gesture. Especially since he was a cop, too. However, she didn't have many options.

It was either go with him or risk using her credit

card to use a rideshare, which likely wouldn't get her all the way to her uncle's place.

"Where are you headed?" Liam asked after they were settled in his SUV.

"Green Lake." She glanced at him. "That's where you live, too, right?"

"Yes, but where in particular?" he asked. "A hotel? What?"

She paused, then admitted, "I'm visiting my uncle Davy McKay for the holiday."

Liam nodded slowly. "I know David. He makes and sells furniture for the Amish Shoppe."

"Yes, he does." She relaxed for the first time in what felt like hours. Not only had Liam rescued her, but he also knew her uncle. The two things together made her feel she might be safe with him.

For now.

"I noticed you don't have any luggage other than your backpack."

Or maybe not. She slanted a glance at Liam. The sheriff was far too observant for her peace of mind. "I should have asked you to grab my small duffel from the trunk, too," she fibbed. "My head was hurting so bad I must have forgotten."

"Understandable." His level tone made it difficult for her to know if he believed her. "Your backpack is really heavy."

"I have my business law textbook in there, along with my computer." This was obviously some sort of not-so-subtle interrogation, but she'd play along. "I took my midterm exam earlier today. It went well, although the grades won't be posted for a couple of days yet."

"Wow, that sounds like a tough class."

"It is, but I enjoy it." That much was true. Only now she was wondering if she'd be back in time to finish the class. She tried not to dwell on that. "Only one more semester to go until I graduate with my bachelor's degree. I've been attending school part-time while working full-time, so it's taken longer than it should." She tried to sound confident, when in reality, she doubted she'd graduate at all. Not unless she figured out who had killed her mother and why she herself was in danger.

Don't go to work—they'll find you there.

Her mother's statement made her shiver.

"Congrats. I'm sure you'll achieve your goal," Liam said, sounding impressed.

Shauna forced a smile. "Thanks. I'm sure I will, too."

It wasn't easy to ignore Liam's intimidating presence beside her. Only a blind woman would be immune to his chiseled good looks. His short, dark hair was a little wavy, his shoulders broad and sturdy. It was clear from the little bit of time they'd spent together that his piercing green eyes didn't miss a thing.

Figured a cop had been the one to see her car sail over the side of the road. Looking back, she still wasn't sure how she'd survived. And with the chilly fall temperatures, she knew she might not have if Liam hadn't rushed to the rescue. She never would have guessed he was in law enforcement, considering the way the responding deputy had spoken to him in such a condescending tone.

Maybe O'Connor was jealous of the fact that Harland was a sheriff while he was only a deputy. Or maybe they hated each other from something else.

None of her business, either way.

She hadn't thought much beyond getting to Green Lake, but now that their destination was only thirty miles ahead, she couldn't help thinking about what she would do here in the middle of nowhere, Wisconsin. Her mother had begged her to be safe, but there was no way she could just hide out with her uncle indefinitely.

No. Somehow, she needed to figure out what was going on. Why her mother had been followed. Murdered.

Why she herself was still a target.

Once again, she regretted her knee-jerk decision to run away from her mother's trailer. Would the officers have placed her in police protection if she'd stayed? Or would they pooh-pooh her mother's fears that Shauna was in danger, too?

The vehicle that sent her over the railing was a pretty large clue that she was.

"I noticed the rear bumper on your Honda was smashed in," Liam said, breaking the silence.

She tensed but tried to sound casual. "Oh, yeah. I was rear-ended a while back while on campus. I didn't have enough money to get my car repaired."

He raised a brow in a way that she felt certain meant he wasn't buying her story.

Not for one hot minute.

"I hope I'm not taking you too far out of your way," she said, changing the subject.

"You're not." He glanced at the rearview mirror

with a slight frown. "Did you happen to notice any-one following you earlier?"

"What?" Her stomach dropped. "Why?" She turned in her seat to glance back through the rear window.

A pair of headlights loomed close. No high beams this time, but still close.

"Hang on," Liam said grimly. He hit the gas, send-ing the SUV lurching forward. She gripped the arm-rest as he waited until the last possible minute to exit the interstate, several miles from their destination.

Shauna found herself holding her breath as he turned right without stopping, still moving well above the posted speed limit.

"I— Are you sure that car was following us?" She didn't see anyone behind them now, which was a relief.

Liam didn't answer right away, but then he pulled off on a side road covered with trees. He maneuvered the vehicle so that they were facing the road, hidden behind an evergreen tree. He cut the engine and turned to face her. "You need to tell me exactly what is going on."

She tried to look innocent, although she never was good at pretending. "I don't know what you mean. I told you, I lost control of my car and went over the guardrail. I know it was very foolish of me to under-estimate the slick roads."

"Try again," he said tersely. "If you've brought danger to Green Lake, I need to know what we're up against."

She swallowed hard. It was difficult not to feel guilty for doing just that. However, he was a cop. Not just any cop, but a sheriff in charge of the entire community. What if he turned around and sent her back to Chicago? She lifted her chin. "Nothing is going on."

"Don't lie to me, Shauna."

She crossed her arms over her thin jacket. "You said you were taking me to my uncle's house. Have you changed your mind? If so, I'll walk from here."

He let out a heavy sigh but then reached out to grab her arm as lights on the road indicated a vehicle was approaching. "Duck down," he whispered.

Even though she figured he was overreacting, she lowered her head. Seconds later, his grip tightened.

"What is it?"

"A large black pickup truck, moving along the road far too slowly."

She gasped, feeling sick to her stomach. The high-beam lights of the vehicle that slammed into her had been higher than her little car and could easily have belonged to a truck.

Was it possible she'd been followed all the way to Green Lake by the same person who'd murdered her mother?

Liam was losing patience with Shauna McKay. He didn't appreciate people who lied to him.

Although, to be honest, he rarely received cooperation from the Amish community in Green Lake, either. Despite his blood relationship with a few members of the community, the Amish were reluctant to involve law enforcement in their concerns. Not to be difficult, but more because they simply viewed themselves as separate from the English world. Shauna's uncle Davy worked for the Amish, so maybe some of his attitude about staying distant from law enforcement had rubbed off on his niece.

"Talk to me, Shauna." He softened his tone. "I can't help you if I don't understand what's going on."

She slowly straightened in her seat. "Did the driver of the truck see us?"

"No. I made sure we were far enough from the road and in the brush." Liam stared at her for a long moment. "I need you to start talking."

"Okay, fine. But not here in the car." She shivered. "It's cold."

He inwardly sighed. "Do you think it's smart to head to your uncle's house?"

"No." She sighed. "I'll need to go to a motel."

Liam didn't like that idea. She'd have to use a credit card, which would be advertising her location to anyone with a few connections.

And the fact that she'd been found here outside Green Lake meant whoever was behind the wheel of the truck had plenty of resources at his or her disposal. Especially since they'd spent several hours in Madison while Shauna had received medical care before making their way north. That they'd located her so soon bothered him.

But she was right—this wasn't the best place to talk. The temperature had dropped, and the landscape would be covered in frost come morning. He started the SUV, then slowly drove back down the narrow road to the main thoroughfare.

"I'll take you to a hotel as long as you let me pay," he said. When she opened her mouth to argue, he held up his hand. "I don't want anyone to track you via your credit card."

She rubbed her head, then reluctantly nodded. "Okay. But as soon as I get in touch with my uncle, I'll borrow his credit card."

Liam hid a smile, as she clearly didn't know how much David had acclimated to the Amish community. While her uncle accepted credit cards for sales, he felt certain David didn't own one himself. Just like he didn't own a cell phone, a car or any other electronic devices.

But that was a problem for tomorrow.

"Keep your eyes open for any sign of a black truck," he said as he took back roads the rest of the way to town.

He had to give her credit for taking his request seriously. She alternated between swiveling around to look behind them and then to the right.

Any doubts he had about her car ending up off the bridge by accident evaporated at just how intensely she watched for impending danger.

It made him wonder if she was guilty of some crime. Otherwise, why not trust the police?

He found a motel five miles outside Green Lake. Thankfully, there was a red vacancy light on in the window. Mid-October still brought tourists to the area, many traveling here to see the beautiful fall colors. He was glad they had a room available.

A place like this might take cash, but learning how Shauna worked full-time while going to school made him wonder how much money she had on her.

He pulled up to the lobby. "Wait here. I'll be back soon."

"Okay." She was still glancing around, searching for any sign of the truck.

The guy behind the desk was more than happy to provide a room with a late checkout. Liam took the key and returned to his SUV.

He drove to room seven and parked. "It's nothing fancy."

"That's fine." Shauna grabbed her heavy backpack. He gave her the key. After she unlocked the door, he followed her inside.

She dropped her backpack on the floor next to the bed. She ran her hand through her hair, and he was struck again by how pretty she was. Older than he'd first thought. When she'd mentioned being a student, he hadn't been sure she was even twenty. Now he thought she was likely around twenty-three or twenty-four.

The flash of attraction was unwelcome. He ruthlessly shoved it aside as he sat in the single chair tucked in the corner of the room.

Shauna dropped onto the edge of the bed. "I'll explain what's going on, under one condition."

He lifted a brow. From where he was sitting, she didn't have any leverage to force his hand. "I'm a cop," he reminded her. "I'm not going to ignore anyone breaking the law."

She stared at him. "I'm not going to ask you to break the law, but I also want you to have an open mind. Because what I'm going to explain is going to sound unbelievable."

He'd been in law enforcement for the past six years—there wasn't much he hadn't heard. "Try me."

"Just after I finished my exam today, my mom called. She sounded paranoid and delusional. Said she'd been followed and firmly believed someone was trying to hurt her. She told me I was in danger, too, and I had to get out of town as soon as possible. To get to Green Lake so my uncle Davy could keep me safe. Then she cried out and the call cut off."

He straightened. "Is that when you decided to drive here?"

"No. First I went to the trailer park where my mom lives. I found her dead, with a butcher knife stuck in her chest. That's when I realized she hadn't been paranoid. Someone had been following her and wanted her dead."

He tried not to sound incredulous. "What did the local police think?"

She lifted her chin. "I didn't stick around long enough to talk to them. You should know that my mother has a criminal record. Mostly drugs and driving under the influence, but I doubted they'd believe her ramblings about being followed and targeted."

He tried not to wince. Fleeing the scene of the crime didn't look good for her. Yet she'd mentioned being in class and on campus, so she likely had an alibi for the time frame of the murder. "Then what happened?"

"I tried to call Davy, but his phone was out of service. I decided to drive to Green Lake, but a vehicle came up behind me on the overpass and rammed into my car. The road was slick to begin with, so it didn't take much to send me spinning out of control."

"I figured you'd been hit from behind, since that smashed bumper looked recent—no rust." He frowned. "I don't understand why you didn't tell Deputy O'Connor about that, though."

Shauna let out a harsh laugh. "I didn't want to say anything to you, either. I have no idea who could have done this, or why. Besides, why do you care? It didn't sound like you and Deputy O'Connor were best friends."

"I barely know the man." Or his brother, but that wasn't important. He decided to change course. "Any chance the black truck that passed us earlier is the same one that ran you off the road?"

"It was dark, so I couldn't see the color of the vehicle, especially with the high-beam lights blinding me." Shauna grimaced. "But the lights were higher than my car, as if they belonged to a truck or maybe an SUV."

Liam didn't believe in coincidences. The way the black truck had been moving slowly made him think the driver was indeed searching for Shauna.

To finish what he'd started on the overpass.

"And you're absolutely sure you have no idea why someone would murder your mother and come after you?"

She slowly shook her head. "I wish I did. Honestly, it would be easier if I could point to someone and say, 'That guy right there is the one responsible.'"

"Think back," he encouraged. "Did you notice anything strange? Anyone following you?"

"I've been doing that throughout the drive here, but there's been nothing out of the ordinary," she insisted.

"You mentioned school, but where do you work?" he asked. Maybe this was related to her job?

"I'm telling you, I live a boring life. I work full-time as an evening desk clerk at a local hotel—much nicer than this one," she added dryly. "I attend school part-time and also help look after my mom…" She looked away, swiping at her face.

The sadness in her eyes tugged at his heart. He knew firsthand what it felt like to see the people you love lying dead. Losing Jerica and Mikey to a terrible car crash had been bad enough.

To find your loved one brutally murdered with a butcher knife to the chest would be far worse.

He scrubbed his hands over his face, fatigue hitting hard. Making the annual trek to Madison to visit his wife and son's grave site had taken an emotional toll.

Now he found himself smack in the middle of another mystery. He stared at the young woman who'd brought danger to his normally quiet town.

"I would respectfully ask that you don't send me back to Chicago," Shauna said. "Please."

He should, but he wouldn't. "You'll be safe here for now." He rose to his feet, knowing tomorrow would bring a new set of challenges. He paused at the door. "Will your uncle David know more about this?"

"I doubt it. We haven't had much contact with him recently." Shauna grimaced. "Mostly because my mom didn't stay in touch. The last time I saw Davy was just over two years ago." She hesitated, then added, "I hope he's not upset by me showing up without warning."

"He won't be." At least, Liam didn't think so. David had adopted many of the Amish ways, which meant he wouldn't turn his back on his niece. Interesting, though, that they hadn't seen each other in over two years. Why had her mother urged Shauna to come here to see him? His tired mind couldn't figure out that puzzle. He opened the door. "I'll see you tomorrow morning. For now, stay put. Lock up and don't open to anyone, okay?"

"Okay."

He left the motel and waited until he heard the lock click before jumping into his SUV.

As he headed home, he tried to avoid thinking about a similar car crash, the one that had taken his wife and son.

And the note Jerica had left behind, indicating their marriage was over and she was moving back to Madison.

Liam sat for a moment behind the wheel of his SUV, knowing he'd never be free of the guilt that accompanied his memories of the past.

THREE

Shauna fell into a troubled sleep. Exhaustion finally overcame the image of her mother's bloody dead body from her mind. But she awoke only four hours later, her head still throbbing, both from the injury and lack of sleep.

The strange surroundings didn't bother her as much as she'd thought. She'd stayed in far worse places while growing up. Shortly after she turned thirteen, her mother had moved them into the Hidden Pines trailer park. At the time, it had been a welcome change. When Shauna had moved out at nineteen, she'd tried to convince her mother to come with her. But her mother had stubbornly refused.

Now her mother was gone forever, and not by something she'd done to herself. But by someone else's hand.

She pushed those thoughts away, although remembering the handsome and all-too-knowing sheriff Liam Harland wasn't a better option. Interesting that he hadn't acted like the cops she'd interacted with over the years. Of course, the cops she'd met had often been arresting her mother because she'd broken the law. Liam had made it clear he wouldn't help her if she'd broken the law. She wasn't sure leaving the scene of a crime counted as breaking the law, but knew he hadn't been happy to hear it.

Yet he hadn't hauled her back to Chicago. Instead, he'd brought her here and even paid for her room. The kind support Liam had displayed had been unexpected.

After washing up in the bathroom, she opened her laptop computer and began to search for information on her mother's murder. It was probably all over the news, but Liam hadn't had the radio on while they'd been driving. And she wasn't sure that Chicago news would reach all the way to Green Lake, Wisconsin.

Ignoring the hunger pains gnawing at her stomach, Shauna connected to the motel's free Wi-Fi. Once the browser loaded, she stared at the search engine, her fingers hovering over the keys. Where should she start?

The local newspaper, the free electronic version of the *Chicago Tribune*, seemed logical. She found herself holding her breath as she scrolled through the news stories. In her experience, former drug addicts who were found dead, even murdered, didn't always make the newspaper. Too many people assumed a victim with her mother's criminal past had gotten what she'd deserved.

Surprisingly, this time it did, although the article was brief.

Forty-year-old Linda Ann McKay died Wednesday night from a fatal stab wound to the chest.

*Two grams of heroin were found nearby, and
police suspect a drug deal gone wrong.*

What? Shauna blinked and read the string of sen-
tences again. Then she curled her fingers into a help-
less fist. Heroin? No way. Her mother had used a lot
of other things, mostly marijuana and speed, but never
anything more potent, like cocaine or heroin.

Especially not heroin. Her mother claimed that the
drug scared her because so many people died from
it. Deaths her mother had witnessed firsthand before
she'd gotten sober.

Had she missed something? Shauna closed her eyes
and forced herself to envision the scene in her mother's
kitchen. No matter how hard she tried, she couldn't
remember seeing either her mom's phone or anything
that looked like drugs.

Because she hadn't noticed? Or because the phone
had been taken and the drugs planted?

That sounded even more paranoid than her mother.

She was tempted to call her study partner Jeff
Clancy to see what he remembered. But that was impossible, since she didn't have a phone or enough
money to buy a new disposable one. Besides, she
doubted Jeff would talk to her. He was likely furious
at the way she'd left him behind to face the police on
his own.

Honestly, she couldn't blame him if he never spoke
to her again.

With a sigh, she returned to the newspaper article,
reading it again, imprinting the words in her mind.

As she scrolled down the page, another article

caught her eye, this one describing a three-alarm fire that had broken out in a small four-family apartment building.

When she saw the address listed was on Davenport Road, her chest tightened. Her apartment was in a four-family building on Davenport Road.

With shaky fingers, she clicked the link to the full article. This one was much longer than the story about her mom's murder.

Firefighters responded to a fire in a four-family apartment building at 2543 North Davenport Road at six o'clock in the afternoon Wednesday. The fire was in full force by the time the fire crews arrived and seemed to have been started in the unit located in the front right corner of the building. All the occupants managed to get out of the structure unharmed, but an investigation into the source of the fire is ongoing. Authorities are searching for Shauna McKay, the renter who lived in the corner unit. At this point, arson is suspected, and the suspicious fire is being thoroughly investigated.

Suspicious fire. The police were looking for her.

The words in the article blurred, and Shauna's chest was so tight she couldn't breathe. While she'd been taking her business law exam, her apartment had been on fire.

A fire that had been started on purpose, mere hours before her mother's murder. A few hours before she was rear-ended off the interstate bypass.

These events all had to be connected in some way.

Impossible to believe it was nothing more than a co-incidence.

Her mother was right. The threat was terrifyingly real.

Shauna was a target, too.

Too bad she had no clue who was behind these attacks—or why.

Unable to sit still, she rose and paced the room. She paused long enough to peer out the window. There was a restaurant about a half mile up the road, across from a gas station.

So close, yet so far.

It was difficult to know how safe she was here. What if the black truck had doubled back? The driver could be going up and down the streets searching for her.

She looked down at herself. The bloodstains she'd missed despite cleaning up in the bathroom weren't that noticeable on her dark blue winter jacket.

Unfortunately, she didn't have any way to disguise herself. No clothes other than what she was wearing, and no possessions other than the items in her back-pack, which contained mostly school and work stuff. Not helpful.

As she watched through the window, a horse-drawn buggy came into view. The woman holding the horse's reins wore a white bonnet on her head and a dark cloak. In the downtown area of Chicago, there were horse-drawn buggy rides you could take to tour the city. Typically, romantic couples or tourists did that sort of thing. She'd personally never been on one. They were ridiculously expensive.

The buggy coming closer didn't look at all like the ones in downtown Chicago. The buggy was plain black, without decoration. She thought about some of the books she'd read about the Amish. Did the Amish live nearby? It was a tad chilly, frost covering the grass and leaves, so she couldn't imagine why anyone would choose to travel by buggy this time of year.

Of course, riding in the buggy would be better than walking, she thought wryly. She glanced around her room, then went over to pack her computer away. After debating ditching the business law book, she stuffed it back inside, slung the backpack over her shoulder and headed for the door.

As she stepped over the threshold, she froze when she saw a dark vehicle turning toward her. The black truck? No, this was an SUV. She caught a glimpse of Liam's scowling face through the windshield.

For some odd reason, his annoyance made her smile.

"Where are you going?" he demanded after pulling up beside her.

"Breakfast." She gestured toward the restaurant down the road. "Why are you here?"

"I told you I'd see you in the morning, and I figured you'd be hungry." He frowned. "Guess it's a good thing I showed up when I did. Jump in. I'll take you someplace nicer."

Personally, she didn't think there was anything wrong with the restaurant nearby, but the chilly wind and the fear of being found by the driver of the black truck convinced her that riding with Liam would be a wise choice.

She double-checked that her motel room door was locked, then hurried over to climb in. "Thanks."

He glanced at her. "You were really going to walk to the restaurant?"

"How else would I get there?" It occurred to her that not having a car would be a problem. Too bad her Honda was nothing but a crumpled wreck.

"Shauna, you need to stay hidden until I can find out more about the black truck and your mother's murder." He frowned. "I'm not sure you should head to your uncle's house, either."

She'd already decided that putting Davy in danger wasn't smart. "That's fine, but I need to talk to him. He needs to know my mother is dead. And that he might be in danger, too."

"I can arrange for the two of you to talk," he agreed.

Her mother's words echoed in her mind. *I need you to leave Chicago right now. Don't go to work—they'll find you there. Find David. He'll keep you safe.*

Did her mother know more about who was following her than she'd let on? How else would she have known Shauna was in danger, too? And sending her to Davy made it sound as if her mother believed he wasn't involved.

In what? She was still clueless. And, worst of all, she couldn't shake the idea she was running out of time.

Liam did his best to tamp down his frustration. Praying hadn't been easy for him since losing Jerica and Mikey, but he couldn't help wondering if God had sent him to the motel in time to prevent something terrible from happening to Shauna.

On some level he admired her independence. Jerica hadn't been like that. She'd bitterly complained when he was forced to work long hours. She'd hated being stuck at home but hadn't wanted to get a job, either. Unfortunately, he'd soon found out Jerica had found someone else to keep her company when he wasn't there—Sean O'Connor, who was Deputy Jason O'Connor's brother, lived in Madison, and he wasn't a cop, but an investment broker. A man she'd wanted to be with far more than Liam.

Our marriage is over. I'm moving back to Madison to be with Sean.

"Where are we going?" Shauna's question drew him from his tumultuous past.

"Rachel's Café. It's in the downtown area of Green Lake."

"It's pretty far from the motel, isn't it?" Shauna asked with a frown.

"You'll need to have a new place to stay anyway." He didn't like having Shauna more than ten miles from where he lived. "We'll find something closer."

Thankfully, she didn't argue. Liam had read the small amount of information about her mother's murder, the news sobering. Clearly, Shauna had told the truth about the knife wound.

Shauna hadn't mentioned the drugs, either because she didn't want him to know or because they hadn't been there. Oddly enough, he was leaning toward the latter. Shauna's car had been pushed off the interstate for a reason—the same reason a black pickup truck had come looking for her.

He'd dug into Linda McKay's criminal history.

There had been busts for possession and possible selling of marijuana and amphetamines, along with several DUIs. Nothing about heroin or cocaine.

His cop instincts were screaming at him that Shauna's mother's murder wasn't related to a drug deal gone bad. That answer was too easy. There was definitely something more going on here.

"This place is cute." Shauna looked pleased with his choice as he parked near the café.

"Green Lake is a nice place to live," he agreed. The café opened early, and he couldn't help but smile when he saw Rachel Miller's dark hair covered in her white *kapp* bustling behind the counter.

"*Ach*, Liam, 'tis certain sure *gut* to see you." Rachel beamed at him.

Shauna glanced between them, no doubt reading more into their acquaintance than there was. "You, too, Rachel. This is a friend of mine, Shauna McKay. Shauna, this is Rachel Miller. Rachel, we'd love breakfast for two, if you don't mind."

"You'll be my first customers of the day," Rachel said with a warm smile.

After they'd placed their order, Liam sat at a small table in the corner of the room, his back to the wall. From his vantage point he could see the door and the traffic going back and forth down Main Street. It wouldn't be easy to identify the black truck from last night, but he wanted to keep an eye out for anything suspicious.

"I had no idea the Amish people worked in town," Shauna said in a hushed tone, cradling her coffee in her hands. "I saw a buggy passing by the motel earlier. There must be an Amish community nearby."

"There is." Liam eyed her over the rim of his coffee cup. "Rachel is a savvy businesswoman. She's recently begun to accept credit card payments."

"Wow." Shauna looked surprised. "I'm sure that has helped her business."

"No, her food is well worth carrying cash," Liam countered. "Even before she changed her policy, customers flocked to her café. And many people who come to the Green Lake area are familiar with the Amish ways and bring plenty of cash, just in case."

"I'm happy for her, then. But when do I get to see my uncle?"

"David works at the Amish Shoppe, a large red barn that houses several Amish businesses." He grinned. "Rachel's Café is one of the few here in town. Most of the other businesses are housed in the barn."

"Davy works with the Amish?"

Liam hesitated. "Yes. You should know he has taken on many of the Amish ways. He's given up his truck, his phone and other electronics. He's living the simple life now."

Her jaw dropped. "You said he was making furniture."

He nodded. "David makes his own furniture and sells it at the Amish Shoppe. But he doesn't use electric tools. He makes everything by hand."

She looked dazed. "He does? I had no idea."

"I wanted you to be prepared for when you see him," he admitted.

"Thanks for telling me." She glanced over in surprise when Rachel brought over their food. "Wow, looks amazing."

"Denke," Rachel said with a gentle smile.

Liam picked up a slice of freshly baked bread. Then, feeling Rachel's eyes on him, he set it down, bowed his head and silently gave a prayer of thanks for their food.

It wasn't that Liam didn't believe in God—he did. But it wasn't easy to comprehend the Lord's plan. Or why his wife and son had died the night she'd decided to leave him.

"I've never tasted anything this good," Shauna raved after sampling her meal. "Incredible."

"See? It's a good thing you trusted me."

Shauna winced. "I'm sorry. It hasn't been easy to do that, Liam. My mother never had good experiences with the police."

"And you?"

She shrugged. "I advocated for my mom, tried hard to get her into treatment programs rather than tossed in jail. So, yeah, my experiences weren't positive, either."

He could understand where she was coming from. "I'm going to do my best to help keep you safe. But you need to do your part." He narrowed his gaze. "No more traipsing out to get breakfast alone."

"It's not like I had your number to call using the motel phone," she protested. "I had no idea you were on your way to pick me up."

"We'll get you a disposable phone so that won't be a problem anymore."

She ate in silence for several moments, clearly enjoying the meal. Then she sat back and sipped her coffee. "You're quick to spend money on someone you barely know."

He shifted uncomfortably in his seat. "It's self-serving to a certain extent. If danger has followed you here, I need to be in the loop of what is happening. This is my town, and I have a responsibility to keep the citizens safe."

"I see." She stared down at her coffee for a moment, then lifted her gaze to his. "I'll do my best to pay you back once this is over. I don't have a lot of money saved up, but I'll give you what I have."

"Shauna, I don't want your money. I want you to trust me enough to tell me who is after you."

"I don't know!" Her tone was sharp. "I promise you, if I did, I'd tell you. It's not like this is my idea of a vacation."

He lifted a hand in surrender. "Okay, I just had to ask. But you must see that the only way I can help you is by trying to stay one step ahead of this guy."

"I know." Her voice was so soft, he could barely hear her.

When they finished eating, he left a generous amount of cash on the table for Rachel. "Ready?"

Shauna nodded and drained her cup.

"Goodbye, Rachel. Have a good day," he called as they made their way toward the door.

"Yes, thanks for breakfast. It was delicious," Shauna added.

"*Wilkom*, Liam and Shauna. Take care of yourselves, too, *ja*?"

"We will." He held the door for Shauna.

"The two of you are awfully friendly," she said as they walked to the SUV.

"She's just a friend," he said firmly, wondering why he wanted Shauna to understand there was nothing romantic going on between them. "Rachel is close friends with my cousin Elizabeth."

Now her gaze was curious. "Elizabeth is Amish, too?"

"Yeah. My parents left the Amish community when I was young, even though they continued to attend church regularly. I think my dad wanted something a little more than what the plain life offered. Elizabeth is the daughter of my mom's sister. We've remained friends despite my career choice."

"What's wrong with being a sheriff?"

"The Amish avoid law enforcement much the way you do, trusting their own processes more than allowing outsiders in." He smiled wryly as he drove through town, back out toward the motel. The Amish Shoppe didn't open for another hour and a half yet, and he needed to officially check Shauna out of the motel.

"It feels a little like I've dropped into an alternate universe," she admitted. "I've read a bit about the Amish people, maybe saw a few come through the hotel where I worked, but I don't know much about them."

"They're good people," Liam said. "As you've noticed, Rachel's cooking is amazing."

Shauna was silent for a moment. "Liam, there's something you need to know."

His gut tensed. "What's that?"

Crack!

What in the world? Liam instinctively swerved, frantically searching the area for the source of the gunfire.

"Get down," he barked, reaching over to push her head lower.

Someone was shooting at them!

He hit the gas, praying they could get away without being hit.

FOUR

Bending at the waist, Shauna braced herself for the worst. Her body began to shake uncontrollably as the SUV sped up and jerked from side to side as Liam attempted to escape.

They were shooting at her this time. Not just attempting to run her off the road.

These people, whoever they were, wanted her *dead*.

Just like her mother.

Why? She couldn't seem to grasp why she'd suddenly become a target. It just didn't make any sense. Tears pricked her eyes, but she held them back.

She wasn't a crier. Growing up the way she did had given her a toughness that others lacked. Then again, never once in her twenty-three years had she feared for her life. Not like this. Not knowing someone wanted her dead.

After what seemed like eons but was likely only fifteen minutes, the vehicle slowed to a normal rate of speed.

"Are you okay?" Liam asked tersely.

She hesitantly lifted her head, scanning the area. "I— Yes. You?"

"Fine. Thankfully, the shooter missed us. I wish I knew exactly where the gunfire came from." He sounded frustrated. "This is my fault. I knew you were in danger, but I didn't expect anyone to fire at us in broad daylight."

"At me." Her voice was soft, but firm. "Not you, Liam. This is all about me."

He glanced sharply at her. "They could have easily shot me, too, Shauna. Thankfully, they missed, but that was too close. And you still don't know why these people have come after you?" He hesitated, then added, "Or why they killed your mother?"

"No." She shrugged helplessly. "I'm not lying. There is no reason I can come up with that would cause this sort of action. No one hated either of us this much."

"Revenge?" He divided his attention between her and the road. She didn't recognize the highway they were on, but then again, she didn't know much of anything about Green Lake.

Other than she'd brought danger to the quaint tourist town.

"Revenge against what?" She blew out a breath. "My mother lived in a low-income trailer, worked as a waitress in a café and barely made ends meet. She had nothing of any value. Everything she owned she bought at secondhand stores. And trust me, it wasn't as if she had some sort of hidden jewel of an antique or anything, either. If she had, she'd have sold it for money toward a car."

"Maybe she did something to someone? During the days she was involved in drugs or drinking?"

"She was sober for the past four years, something she was really proud of. That would be a long time for someone to nurse a grudge. Besides, abusing marijuana, amphetamines and alcohol aren't exactly bigtime crimes."

"I noticed she had a couple of citations for DUI."

Her cheeks burned with shame, even though her mother's actions weren't her fault. Still, it was clear Liam had checked out her mother's background. And likely Shauna's, too. "Yes, but she didn't hurt or kill anyone, thankfully. And she did her time. Surprisingly, being held in jail for the weeks after her third DUI was the first step of her becoming sober." Shauna didn't expound on how hard she'd worked to get her mother into rehab—no easy task unless you had a lot of money to spend.

Which they hadn't.

She'd worked extra hours at a restaurant in addition to her hours at the hotel to help pay the fees, almost failing her class because she'd worked several sixteen-hour days without having any time to study.

The sacrifice had been worth it, as her mother had stayed clean. Looking back, she realized her mother's paranoia hadn't become obvious until the past few weeks or so.

What had changed? She wished she'd taken her mother's rambling concerns more seriously.

"Shauna?"

"What?" Her tone was sharp, and she inwardly winced. None of this was Liam's fault.

"I need you to think back on the weeks before your mother's murder. See if you can come up with anything that may give a hint about why this happened."

"I've done nothing but go over things in my mind. All I can say for sure is that my mother seemed more paranoid over the past four weeks. She claimed she was being followed and that she was in danger."

"Did she say anything to indicate it was a man following her? A woman? Young or old?" Liam pressed.

She rubbed her temples. "I had the impression it was a man that had raised concern." She did her best to think back to those frantic phone calls. "I think her exact words were 'I saw him following me from the café to the bus stop.'"

"Bus stop?"

Shauna waved an impatient hand. "My mother didn't drive because of those DUIs you mentioned. She normally walked to work, unless the weather was bad. I think the day she called me we had a big rainstorm, so she'd taken the bus."

Liam didn't say anything for a long moment. "I need to call the local police, find out what they've discovered so far. Maybe the detective on the case has some additional information that would help us figure things out."

Her stomach knotted. "They'll want me to come back to Chicago, maybe even arrest me for leaving the scene of a crime."

His fingers tightened on the steering wheel. "Technically, you didn't break the law by leaving Chicago, but the police will for sure want to talk to you as a person of interest. I'm the sheriff here. I can't just ignore an attempted murder."

"Okay, then drop me off at the closest bus station. Once I'm out of the area, you can call the Chicago police. You can relay to them everything I've explained to you, but I'll be long gone before they can find me."

"Shauna…" He sighed and shook his head. "Give me some time to consider my options. I don't want you to leave, not yet. The closest Greyhound bus depot is in Fond du Lac, which is thirty miles east of here."

Thirty miles would be a long walk. Green Lake wasn't a big town—at least, from the little bit she'd seen of it. Did this place even have rideshare services available?

Did it matter? No phone and no credit card meant no way to call for one. Or to pay for the bus ticket, either.

Scary how dependent she'd become on modern conveniences.

Maybe Uncle Davy would drive her to Fond du Lac? Then she grimaced, remembering how Liam had mentioned her uncle giving up all electronics, including a car. At this point, she wouldn't argue with taking a horse-drawn buggy. Would asking that sort of favor put him in danger?

"When is the last time you saw my uncle?" She twisted in her seat to face Liam. "I stayed away last night to protect him, but now I'm worried. What if he's a target, too?"

"I saw David a few days ago, when I stopped in to visit my cousin Elizabeth." Liam frowned. "But why would David be in danger?"

"I don't know!" She tried to rein in her panic. "I

don't understand any of this, but I need to know he's okay. I've already lost my mother. I can't bear it if something happens to Davy…"

Liam nodded and put a reassuring hand on her arm. "Try to stay calm. We can swing by his place later. Right now, I need to come up with a place for you to stay. And find another vehicle to use."

"Another vehicle?" Realization dawned. "You think the shooter has your license plate?"

"I can't afford to assume he doesn't." Liam's expression was grim. "It's unusual, though, that anyone would have a cavalier attitude toward shooting at a cop."

"Maybe they don't know who you are. Which is a good thing, as I hate knowing you're involved in this." She swallowed hard. What she needed was extra cash and a way out of town. Having grown up in a variety of low-income apartments and trailers, it wouldn't be the first time she'd had to live from paycheck to paycheck.

Once she knew her uncle was okay, she'd leave. Her mother had claimed Davy would keep her safe, but Linda hadn't indicated that Davy knew anything about why someone might be following her.

Why that same person had killed her.

Shauna stared blindly out at the unfamiliar surroundings along the incredibly rural highway. She didn't want to be the reason anyone was harmed.

If that meant going off to live under the radar and completely on her own, then so be it.

Kicking himself for being lax, Liam continued heading farther into the north woods. The town of

Green Lake was surrounded by several parks, and he'd chosen one at random as a place to go so they could talk.

Logically, he knew he should haul Shauna in. Not because she'd done anything illegal. Her leaving the scene of a crime wasn't something that would send her to jail, but it would make her look guilty. She really needed to be interviewed about what she knew or what she'd seen.

Too bad, because having her in jail would be a good way to keep her safe.

Her request to go to a bus station had surprised him. Was she really willing to head out to a strange city to start over? That was something he couldn't imagine. After Jerica and Mikey had died, he'd wanted nothing more than to head out of town, but he couldn't leave his life—his career—behind.

Besides, leaving wouldn't have prevented the memories from looping over and over in his mind. Going back through every argument they'd had, wishing he could respond differently.

He pulled into the park and then shut down the SUV. Normally, he found the silence out here peaceful.

But not when he could feel the tension radiating off Shauna.

"Okay, I won't call the Chicago police."

She winced. "I don't want you to get in trouble for helping me out."

Her concern for him was heartwarming. It had been a long time since he'd felt that anyone personally cared about him. "The cops won't arrest you, Shauna. You must have been seen on campus during the time frame of your mother's murder. Besides, you wouldn't be the first person to get scared and leave when stumbling across a murder. I don't want you to worry about getting arrested, okay?"

"They'll want to talk to me."

"Yeah, they will. As I said, you're a person of interest. And you not talking to them will only make it seem as if you're hiding something."

"I'm not." She dragged her blue eyes to his. "I read the article, Liam. There were no drugs at the trailer when I was there. And no sign of her phone, either."

He nodded slowly. "Looks like someone is going to great lengths to cover their tracks."

"Well, someone should mention to that same person how shooting at the local sheriff isn't the way to do that."

Her sass made him grin. There was something so blunt and forthright about Shauna. She clearly didn't put up with any nonsense and she certainly didn't play games, not the way some women did.

The way Jerica sometimes had.

Don't go there. He cleared his throat. "What else do you remember about the crime scene?"

She closed her eyes and turned away. "So much blood…"

"I'm sorry." He rested his hand on her arm. "I don't mean to make you relive the awful memory."

"I know." She lightly covered his hand with hers, sending an electrical jolt zipping up his arm. He quickly dropped his hand, doing his best to ignore his racing heart. "I don't remember anything else, though. It was all so surreal…"

"Hey, it's okay." He attempted a reassuring smile.

"The Chicago PD may have gotten some DNA or fingerprints from the killer. But I won't know about those things until I talk to them."

"I told you to go ahead and call them, after I'm gone."

"I'd rather you stay where I can help protect you." He found it difficult to explain why he wanted— needed—her to stay. "The danger is already here in Green Lake, Shauna, and you leaving won't change that. Give me a chance to arrest the guy responsible."

Indecision crossed her features. After several long moments, she said, "I'll think about it. But for now, I'd really like to check on my uncle Davy."

The last thing he wanted to do was to drive to David's small house outside town. If the gunman had gotten his license plate, then that wouldn't be a smart thing to do.

He hadn't been joking about getting a different vehicle. There was an unmarked car at the sheriff's department he could use for a few days. It would mean heading back into town, but that couldn't be helped.

"Okay, first we get a different vehicle. Then we can find your uncle."

"You'll take me to his house?"

"Not yet." He glanced at the time. It was quarter past nine o'clock in the morning. The Amish Shoppe didn't open until ten, but he knew David sometimes went in first thing to get work done. The workshop where he made his furniture by hand was located behind the storefront. "He'll probably be at the Amish Shoppe, so we'll go there first. Okay?"

She nodded. "Thanks."

For what? Nearly getting her killed? He cast his

gaze around the mostly empty parking lot. As the sun raised the temperature, visitors would arrive soon to take in the stunning fall foliage. Having tourists around was great for the city, but not as good for trying to identify someone who didn't belong.

Someone with murder on their mind.

He put the SUV in Reverse and took a long circular route back into Green Lake, coming in on the opposite side of town from the way they'd left.

Pulling into the small parking lot next to the sheriff's department, which shared a building with the courthouse and jail, he turned to Shauna. "Wait here for a minute. I need to stop inside to grab the keys to the silver sedan."

She nodded. "I see it."

"We'll head over to the Amish Shoppe from here." He hoped she wouldn't try to leave—not that she'd get very far on foot.

Liam strode inside, nodded at Garrett Nichol, his chief deputy, and hurried to grab the keys off his desk.

"Where are you headed?" Garrett asked.

"I'll fill you in later." He wasn't trying to be evasive but didn't want to linger, either. "Put the deputies on alert, though. Someone was taking wild shots about six miles outside the city limits to the west."

"Hunters?" Garrett asked.

"I don't think so." He glanced at his watch. "Give me another thirty minutes. Then I'll give you the full story, okay?"

"Understood."

Liam hurried back outside, relieved to see Shauna

was still waiting in the SUV. He crossed over to open her door.

"I need my backpack," she said, pulling it from behind the passenger seat.

Once they were settled in the sedan, he drove out of town toward the large refurbished barn that housed the Amish Shoppe. The space had been sectioned off into smaller bays, each showcasing Amish wares—anything from homemade food items, like jams, jellies, bread and butter, to the handmade quilts his cousin Elizabeth sold and, of course, David McKay's furniture. He'd personally had his eye on the four-post bed frame David had set up in his showroom.

"Wow, this place is bigger than I thought," Shauna said as the red barn came into view.

"You'd be surprised at how well they do," he agreed. "People come from all over, as far south as Chicago and west from the Twin Cities, to buy Amish-made items."

The parking lot was empty, because it was too early for customers to be there. And the Amish didn't drive cars. Most of them walked or found a ride via a horse and buggy to get to and from work.

"Ready?" he asked as he shifted the sedan into Park.

She reached for her backpack, but he put a hand out to stop her. "Do you mind if I ask why you're lugging that heavy business law book around?"

"I don't know." She grimaced. "I suppose it's silly, huh? It's not like I'll be able to return to my class." The despair on her features tugged at him.

"You promised to give me a little time. Once I arrest this guy, you should be able to go back home."

"What home?"

He stared at her. "Oh, I didn't realize you lived with your mother at the trailer."

"I didn't." She sighed heavily. "That's what I was going to tell you before the gunfire rang out."

"Tell me what?"

"Yesterday, a fire broke out in my apartment building. The police claim the cause is arson, and they're looking for me because the fire apparently started in my apartment."

His jaw dropped in surprise. Just when he thought he could trust her. "Did you set the fire?"

She scowled. "No, I did not. From what I can tell, the fire started while I was in class. So much for believing in me, huh?" She thrust open the door and jumped out of the sedan, lugging the overweight backpack with her.

Liam hurried to catch up. This latest news was an unexpected and unwelcome twist. Something she should have mentioned much sooner.

Why would someone burn down her apartment building?

And what else was Shauna McKay keeping from him?

FIVE

Her anger was unreasonable, yet she couldn't seem to help herself. It wasn't her fault shots had been fired when she was about to tell him about the fire in her apartment. Yanking on the Amish Shoppe door, she frowned when it didn't move.

The place was locked. She spun to face Liam, anger spiking again. "I thought you said we would see Uncle Davy."

Liam arched a brow. For some odd reason, his calm demeanor only annoyed her more. "We will. He's usually here early. His place is around the back—there's a private doorway leading into his workroom. This way."

Shifting the weight of her pack, she followed Liam around the building. Up close the barn seemed even larger, and she liked that it was painted a bright, cheery red. They walked all the way down to the end of the barn, and when they turned the corner, she saw the door Liam mentioned. He reached it first, knocking sharply.

A moment later, the door opened, and her uncle peered out. "Liam, is there a problem?" Then Uncle Davy's gaze landed on her. "Shauna? Is that you?"

She was so relieved to see him alive and well that tears welled in her eyes. She took the two steps toward him and hugged him tight.

"Ah, Shauna," he murmured. "It's really good to see you."

She hadn't realized how much she needed to be with her family. The only family member she had left. After a long moment, she released her uncle. "I'm glad you're okay."

"Okay?" Davy looked questioningly between her and Liam before gesturing to the door. "I have a feeling this isn't just a social visit. Come in. I have fresh coffee."

Liam stepped back, gesturing for her to go in first.

Stepping into the workroom was like taking a trip back in time. No power tools were anywhere to be seen, but there were various saws, sandpaper and other tools that could be operated by hand. An unfinished baby cradle stood in the center of the room, and she was amazed at how beautifully simple it was.

Not that she imagined needing one for herself. She didn't trust men enough to let them get close. Especially not after finding out the magnitude of the lies Eric had told her. She'd given that man a year of her life, believing they had something special.

But their relationship had been nothing but a farce. The man had been married the entire time.

Shame still burned at how she'd been duped. She pushed it away with an effort to focus on the present.

"You do amazing work, Uncle Davy," she said in awe. "I remember you worked construction years ago, but this seems very different."

"Yes, it certainly is," Davy agreed. "But I find the work much more rewarding. Come, I have a small table and chairs in the kitchenette. We'll have coffee while you explain what brought you all the way here from Chicago."

She braced herself for instant coffee and the horrific story she had to tell him about his sister. But the coffee wasn't instant—he poured it out of an old-fashioned coffeepot heated on the wood-burning stove. Davy gave her and Liam mugs of coffee, then added some to his own. They sat at the table, one that she felt certain Davy had made himself right here in this very workshop.

"Shauna?" Davy reached across the table to take her hand. "This is about your mother, isn't it?"

"Yes." Fresh tears welled. "She was murdered, Davy. Brutally murdered, and the same person who killed her has come after me, too."

"Murdered?" Davy looked shocked. "I don't understand. I assumed she had…" His voice trailed off, but she knew what he'd meant.

It was more likely that her mother would have died from alcohol or drug abuse. Not murder.

"When's the last time you spoke to your sister?" Liam asked.

Davy shook his head slowly. "I'm sorry to say it's been over two years. I gave up my phone, my internet, all ties to the English world. I told Linda that was my plan." His expression looked pained. "She laughed and told me I was stupid for making my life harder than it needed to be."

Shauna winced. "I'm sorry she wasn't supportive."

"It was more that she didn't understand." Davy

shrugged. "I don't hold that against her. This is the life I've chosen. A way of living that makes me feel closer to God."

There was no denying that her uncle looked younger than his thirty-six years. Maybe that was what finding peace did for a person.

Too bad she didn't see much peace in her future.

"Shauna, why do you think you're in danger?" Davy asked.

"Someone ran me off the highway, and since I've arrived here in Green Lake, that same person, so I assume, has taken shots at me."

"What?" Davy looked stunned. "Liam, you must keep Shauna safe!"

"I'm trying, but your niece is being rather stubborn." Liam shot her a pointed glance. "Claims she wants to get out of town, go off-grid."

"I don't want anyone to be hurt because of me." She sighed and looked at her uncle. "Especially you, Davy. I'm really glad to find you're safe."

"I don't see why anyone would come after me," Davy said. "I haven't been involved in Linda's life for many years." He turned toward Liam. "Shauna's plan to go off-grid isn't the worst idea. Especially if she was somewhere no one would think to look for her."

For a moment the two men exchanged a knowing glance. Then Liam slowly nodded. "I get what you're saying. And it's an interesting thought, David."

"What idea?" She frowned at them. "I don't understand what you're talking about."

"I should discuss this with Elizabeth," Liam said without answering her question. "It's a lot to ask, and she may not be in favor of helping. I hate to take advantage of our family relationship, but I'm not sure I have a better way to keep Shauna safe."

"I think Elizabeth will agree," Davy said. "Especially if Shauna helps look after her mother-in-law, Ruth. Elizabeth could use some help, as Ruth's health has been failing a bit."

"Wait a minute. Are you saying what I think you're saying?" She wanted to believe she misunderstood. "You can't possibly expect me to live with the Amish."

"If Elizabeth agrees, yes," Liam said.

"No way. Not happening." She finished her coffee and pushed the cup away. "If I could borrow some money for a bus ticket, I'll get out of your hair."

"Shauna, please listen to reason. Wearing Amish clothes is the perfect disguise." Davy ignored her flat-out refusal. "The *kapp* will cover your hair, and the skirt and apron will cover the rest of you. You'll blend in, rather than standing out among the others."

"You want me to dress like the Amish? Live like them? Without electricity? Without my computer? Without knowing anything about them?" She knew her voice was rising, but she couldn't seem to hold back. "Have you lost your mind?"

"Think of it as going off-grid while staying here to help me catch the man responsible for murdering your mother," Liam said.

He'd made a good point, one she couldn't entirely discount. Still, it was difficult to stem the rising panic. "I'm not sure I can do this," she said. "From what you've described, the Amish life is so different…"

"They're good people, Shauna." Davy's voice held

a note of underlying steel, warning her that he wasn't going to be easily swayed. "They've welcomed me into their church, and I know Elizabeth could use some help. Her husband passed away last year, and while she's managing fine with the help of the community, another helping hand can't hurt. Besides, it won't be forever. Just a few days, maybe a week or two at the most."

A week or two? Shauna wasn't entirely sure she'd last twenty-four hours.

"We can't move forward until I discuss this with Elizabeth," Liam said firmly. "She may not want to participate in harboring an English woman in her home, and I won't force her."

"She'll be in soon," Davy said. "When the shops open for business."

"I'll talk to her." Liam turned to face her. "Is that okay with you, Shauna?"

She reluctantly nodded, knowing it was wrong to secretly hope Elizabeth would flat-out refuse to participate in their wild scheme.

David's idea was so simple, Liam knew he should have come up with it himself. Maybe Shauna didn't look thrilled with the plan, but she'd get over it.

Her safety was the most important factor here. He would feel much better if she stayed in the Green Lake area long enough for him to arrest the gunman.

"What are we going to do to keep Uncle Davy safe?" Shauna abruptly asked. "Since I have no idea why my mother was murdered, or why someone has targeted me, I don't think we should assume that Davy isn't in danger, too."

"You're right," Liam agreed.

David waved a hand, downplaying Shauna's concern. "I haven't seen anything suspicious, but I can sleep here in the workshop if you think that will help. I have done that in the past while working late."

"I think it's a good idea for you to sleep here for the next few days." Liam finished his coffee. "And keep your eyes open for danger. We already know the killer followed Shauna here from Chicago. It's no stretch to assume they'll learn about your relationship as uncle and niece."

"See? This is exactly why I should leave town!" Shauna's voice held a note of exasperation.

"Your leaving doesn't ensure David's safety," Liam countered.

Her shoulders slumped, and she sighed heavily and nodded. "Yeah, yeah. I get it."

Liam stood and moved through the workshop toward the showroom area. Looking through the glass doors, he could see several of the Amish had come in to set up for the day.

David joined him. "Perhaps it would be better for me to ask Elizabeth. Shauna is my niece."

Liam hesitated. He suspected David had feelings for his cousin, and he was okay with that. But he didn't want this request to hurt their relationship, either.

"I'll do it," Liam said. "She'll probably be more likely to tell me no if she truly doesn't want to do this."

"That's my point," David argued. "Best if we both put pressure on."

"Look, if Elizabeth doesn't feel comfortable bringing me to her home, there is a plan B." Shauna spoke up. "I'll borrow money to get out of town. It's as simple as that."

He sighed inwardly. Shauna's obstinate attitude was wearing thin. Catching a glimpse of Elizabeth in her dark dress and white *kapp* walking toward her quilt store, which was located adjacent to David's furniture shop, he unlocked the glass doors and stepped through to meet her.

"*Gut* morning, Liam. What brings you here today?" Elizabeth's large brown eyes turned somber. "Nothing criminal, I hope."

"Sort of," he acknowledged. After she unlocked the door to her shop, he followed her inside. To his surprise, Shauna joined him. He shot her a questioning glare, but she ignored it, making it clear she was sticking around. Considering this was all about her, there was no point in arguing. "Elizabeth, this is David's niece, Shauna McKay. Shauna, my cousin Elizabeth Walton."

"*Sehr gut* to meet you," Elizabeth said warmly. "I can see the family resemblance, especially around the eyes, *ja*?"

"I— Uh, thanks." Shauna shifted to look around the shop, where Elizabeth had dozens of quilts on display. "Your quilts are beautiful. I'm quite impressed."

"*Denke*, but my fingers are guided by God." Elizabeth looked from Shauna back to him. "I can see you need help, Liam. What is it?"

He decided to get straight to the point. "I'm afraid Shauna is in grave danger. Her mother, David's sister, was murdered, and the killer has come after Shauna now, too. I know it's asking a lot, but I was hoping you might be willing to take Shauna in for a few days. She could help with caring for your mother-in-law or any other daily chores."

Elizabeth met his gaze and nodded slowly. "I see. You are asking for me to help Shauna hide in plain sight."

"Yes." He squashed the flash of guilt. "I don't want to put you or your mother-in-law in danger. The people looking for Shauna would never suspect her to be living with the Amish. And it would only be for a few days, just long enough for me to find the killer."

"Elizabeth, I will completely understand if you say no," Shauna said. "I'm afraid I don't know anything about being Amish. Other than I saw an Amish woman earlier this morning, driving a horse and buggy down the road."

"*Ach*, 'tis a simple life, nothing more. And of course I am happy to help, Liam," she agreed without hesitation. Her dark gaze turned toward David, hovering in the doorway. Liam didn't think he imagined the hint of longing there. "Shauna is *wilkom* to stay in my home for as long as needed."

"Thank you, cousin," Liam said. "I will do everything in my power to keep you and Shauna safe."

"*Ach*, I have no fear. God is with us." Elizabeth shrugged off his concern. "However, I will need to open my shop soon. I may not be able to take Shauna to my home until later."

"That's fine," Shauna hastened to reassure her. "I'll stick around to help Uncle Davy."

Liam suspected that Shauna wanted to put off dressing as Amish for as long as possible. A plan he didn't necessarily agree with. "I can drive you both back to the house, Elizabeth," he offered quickly. "It wouldn't take long to get spare clothes for Shauna."

"I thought the Amish didn't ride in cars?" Shauna asked with a frown. "You shouldn't make Elizabeth do something that goes against her religion."

"We don't own or drive them," Elizabeth agreed. "But our choice to live a simple life doesn't absolutely forbid us from riding in them on occasion." She hesitated, then nodded. "Okay, but we need to be quick. I don't want to open late and miss a potential sale."

"I'll keep my showroom closed so I can run your quilt shop, Elizabeth," David offered. "It's no trouble."

"Denke," Elizabeth said with a nod.

The trip to Elizabeth's home didn't take long. Shauna looked around curiously as she followed Liam's cousin inside. Moments later, the two women emerged, Shauna dressed in a plain dark blue dress and white apron, her hair covered with a white *kapp*. The disguise didn't cover the thin trio of stitches in her forehead, but that was okay.

Shauna didn't look happy, but she didn't complain, either. He personally thought she was attractive no matter what she wore. Especially her expressive blue eyes. The woman was trouble with a capital *T*, but he couldn't help being relieved she was going along with their plan.

Not just because he wanted to get the killer behind bars. But on a personal level, too.

Ridiculous, really, as he had no intention of going down the relationship path. He'd failed at one marriage, losing the two people he loved more than anything. Even though his wife hadn't loved him the same way, considering she'd broken their vows and found someone new.

A man with more money and a job with regular hours. Something Liam couldn't offer her.

No, he wasn't anxious to repeat that experience. One colossal failure was more than enough. Still, he couldn't help but smile when Shauna looked at him.

"You look great, Shauna," he said as he opened the back door for Elizabeth. "No one will recognize you now."

"I barely recognize myself," Shauna said dryly, tugging on the *kapp*.

After driving Shauna and Elizabeth back to the Amish Shoppe, he escorted them back to the quilt store. There was one customer examining quilts with David hovering nearby, and Elizabeth quickly hurried over.

"Are you sure you're okay hanging out here all day?" he asked Shauna.

"Better than sitting in Elizabeth's house, don't you think?" Shauna gestured to where David was opening his showroom. "This will give me some time to get to know my uncle and to help out."

"Okay." His phone buzzed, and he quickly answered it. "Sheriff Harland."

"It's Garrett. Where are you?"

"At the Amish Shoppe. Why?"

"You're going to want to head out to Sunset Park, ASAP."

The somber tone made his gut clench. "On my way."

He turned and strode quickly through the midmorning crowd that had already gathered. "Why? What's going on?"

"A group of fishermen found a dead body."

"What?" Liam quickened his pace. "A drowning?" Even as he asked the question, he knew it was foolish. No one went swimming in Green Lake, the deepest lake in the state—other than Lake Michigan—in the middle of October.

"No, boss. It's a homicide."

"I'll be there in five minutes." Liam shoved his phone in his pocket and jumped behind the wheel. He wished he had his official SUV, as there were no lights or sirens in the silver sedan.

Traffic was light, though, so he didn't really need them. He pulled in beside Garrett's squad car and hurried over to the shoreline.

Another deputy was standing with Garrett, near the body that had been dragged from the water. As Liam approached, he noticed the victim was a slightly overweight male, roughly in his midthirties.

He was about to ask why Garrett had deemed this a homicide, but then Liam noticed the bullet wound in the victim's head.

Liam blew out a breath. "How long do you think he's been in the water?"

"Not sure. He's not that bloated, so it may not have been for long," Garrett responded. "We'll need to spread out, see if we can find blood evidence. There's no blood or any other indication of foul play around here, so the murder didn't happen in this location."

Liam thought about the gunfire he'd heard earlier,

in a location that was well on the other side of the lake. Was it possible the gunfire they'd heard hadn't been meant for Shauna?

Had the shooter been aiming at this man instead?

He knelt beside the body, raking his keen gaze over him. Midthirties, out of shape, the guy's face was that of a stranger. Yet Liam felt certain this murder could be related to whatever was going on with Shauna and her mother.

Danger had definitely struck his quiet tourist town, and he didn't like it one bit.

SIX

Wearing Amish clothing felt strange and sometimes unwieldy. Shauna kept thinking people were staring at her, until she realized those same people were staring at all the Amish.

One thing Liam had gotten right—at this moment, she was just one of the many Amish women, not Shauna McKay from Chicago.

As much as she hated to admit it, she felt safe. Being part of the crowd had its advantages.

"Shauna, would you mind manning the showroom while I work?" Davy had opened the glass doors so potential shoppers could browse.

"Of course. I'm happy to do that." She glanced around in confusion. "I don't see a credit card machine or cash register. How would you like me to ring up sales?"

He smiled. "We accept cash and credit card payments but use a manual process of obtaining the information. There's a ledger here, and some carbon-paper invoices as well." He pulled out a clipboard. "You write up what they've purchased and the amount of cash you've received. Then you give them a copy. I keep the original for my records and would ask you to record the sale in the ledger."

"Okay, I guess I can handle that." She smiled wryly. "Who am I to argue with your process?"

Davy hesitated. "I know the simple life seems harsh to you, but it's just the opposite. When you give up technology and the distractions that go along with it, you begin to understand what is important. Like having a closer relationship with God and, of course, with your family."

A flash of guilt hit hard. Why hadn't she and her mother made time to visit Davy in the past couple of years? Sure, she was busy with school and work, but that didn't mean they couldn't have made a trip up to Green Lake over a long weekend, if they'd wanted to.

They should have. If her mother hadn't wanted to come, Shauna could have made the trip herself. She grimaced. "I'm sorry."

Davy shook his head and wrapped his arm around her shoulders. "I didn't say that to make you apologize. I only wanted you to understand my position. Why I've chosen to live the simple life."

She hugged him back. "I know, and I can tell it suits you. You look happy and content, Davy. Go on, now. You said you had work to do."

He moved through the showroom and the doorway that separated the two spaces. He closed the door, and for a moment she thought the sound of the tools would interfere with the shopping experience, but then she remembered there were no power tools.

It was all so mind-boggling, yet as she meandered through the showroom looking at various pieces, she couldn't deny her uncle did amazing work. She stopped at another baby cradle, running her fingers along the smooth, polished wood.

Babies. She'd once thought she might have a family of her own, but that was until she'd learned the truth about Eric. From that point forward, she'd refused to even think about children as part of her future.

What would it feel like to be loved by someone? To have a family? She didn't think that was her path in life, yet she couldn't seem to move away from the baby cradle, sending it swinging back and forth.

Wait a minute. She turned and looked over to Elizabeth's quilt shop. Hadn't there been a baby quilt in there? She hurried over to find Elizabeth.

"Shauna, is something wrong?"

"No, everything is fine. I—just had an idea, though. Could I display one of your baby quilts on Uncle Davy's cradle? I think it would draw the shopper's eye, don't you?"

Elizabeth brightened. "Certain sure it would. *Komm.* Which do you think is best?"

Shauna ran her gaze over the various quilts. They were all beautiful. But the one done in pale greens and yellows was her favorite, so she gestured to it. "This one."

"Sehr gut." Elizabeth took the quilt from the rack and handed it to her. "We could use the marriage quilt to drape over the bed frame, too."

Why not? "That's a great idea. I'll borrow both of them. Thanks, Elizabeth."

"Denke. And I believe there is a customer coming to David's showroom now."

Shauna hurried over to tuck the baby quilt into the

cradle, then draped the wedding quilt over the bed frame. She noticed several people came in and went straight to those two areas to examine first. But she was disappointed when she didn't get an immediate sale. As the morning marched on, several customers browsed, a young couple and an older gentleman, yet she still didn't sell anything.

Her mind went back to the *Chicago Tribune* articles she'd found, the one describing how heroin had been found in her mother's trailer and the one mentioning the suspicious fire that had destroyed her apartment. It didn't make sense that someone had set her apartment on fire. What was the point? Especially when she was in class at the time? It wasn't as if the arsonist had intended to frame her for the crime.

Not that it mattered one way or the other. The sobering reality was that she didn't have a home to go back to.

Knowing the fire started in her apartment meant all her possessions, other than the backpack she'd brought with her, were gone. Not that she'd owned anything of value, but the cheap furniture, clothes and other memorabilia were still hers.

Now she had nothing.

A wave of despair hit hard. She struggled to push it back, especially when the couple who had been browsing approached. "We're interested in buying the cradle and the quilt."

"That's wonderful." Shauna noticed Elizabeth hovering and sent her a reassuring smile. She was grateful her marketing strategy had finally worked.

Too bad she couldn't turn her personal life around as easily.

* * *

When the medical examiner arrived at the lake-shore, Liam was surprised to find that the estimated time of death was earlier than he'd thought. "Are you sure?"

"The cold water likely helped preserve the body, but the lack of fish bites makes me think this man died a while ago and was dumped in the water recently."

He frowned. "I heard a gunshot earlier today. It's highly likely this guy was the victim."

"I don't agree." The medical examiner was shared between Green Lake County and Fond du Lac County. As their crime rate was so low, especially when it came to homicides, they didn't have a coroner of their own. "See how much blood has pooled along the victim's back side? He was shot and left lying on his back for several hours before being tossed into the lake. According to your officers, the actual site of the shooting isn't nearby."

"True." Liam had sent Garrett to investigate the area where he'd heard the earlier gunfire, six miles to the west of town. Only now he doubted that had been the right thing to do. "I appreciate any additional information you can give us."

"Did you take his fingerprints?" the medical examiner asked. "Knowing his name would be helpful."

"Yes. I'm heading into town to run them now." Liam had been reluctant to leave the area until the doctor arrived. He gestured to one of his deputies, Jake Sanders, who had just finished his rookie year. "I need you to stay here for a while. I'm heading back to the station."

"Got it." Jake shot a glance at the victim. "Any idea who did this?"

"Not yet." It wasn't his first homicide, but it was Jake's, so he understood the young man's concern. "Don't worry. We'll find him."

"Yes, sir."

Liam turned to head back to the silver sedan. He was anxious to get the victim's fingerprints into the system. There had been no wallet or ID in the guy's pockets.

If the guy wasn't in the system, then they'd have to canvass the area to see if anyone recognized him. No easy task with only a dead man's face to show them.

Liam kept a wary eye out for any sign of being followed as he drove back into town. He couldn't ignore the fact that the medical examiner might be right about the victim's time of death.

Which meant the danger to Shauna was still front and center.

He believed she was safe with David at the Amish Shoppe, partially because of being surrounded by people, but more so because no one would recognize her in Amish dress. He owed his cousin for doing this favor, and he'd happily buy another quilt or two to repay her kindness.

At the station, he ran the dead man's fingerprints through the system. As he was waiting for a response, his phone rang. "Hey, Garrett, find anything?"

"No sign of the crime scene, but I found an older man who also heard the wild gunfire you described. Two shots, he said, both taking place at around eight o'clock this morning."

"Yeah, thanks. I appreciate knowing someone else heard the gunfire I did. Unfortunately, it's not the right time frame for our victim's murder. The medical examiner said that took place several hours ago, maybe even last night."

"That makes sense," Garrett admitted. "Besides, I doubt it would have taken two gunshots to kill our John Doe. The bullet wound in the temple looks to have been done up close and personal."

Liam sat back in his chair. "You're right. The lake water might have washed away some of the gunpowder residue, but maybe not all of it. And not the powder burns, either. I'm sure the medical examiner will let us know what he finds."

"Roger that." There was a pause before Garrett said, "You promised to fill me in on what's going on."

"Meet me here at the station," Liam told him. "No point in continuing to look for the scene of the crime. The murder could have happened anywhere."

"I'll be there soon," Garrett promised.

Liam sighed heavily when the search result in AFIS, the Automated Fingerprint Identification System, came up empty. Their victim didn't have a criminal background, nor one in law enforcement or as a government worker.

When Garrett arrived, Liam gave his chief deputy the bad news. "We don't have an identity for this guy."

"Figures." Garrett dropped into the chair beside Liam's desk. "What's going on? What's with the gunfire this morning? And why are you driving the undercover car?"

Liam took a moment to fill Garrett in on how

Shauna McKay had found her mother murdered, had been run off the road, had her apartment set on fire and had been followed into town by someone driving a large black pickup truck.

Garrett whistled. "Not good. I'm glad she's managed to survive all of that. But how is the victim we found connected to her?"

"I have no idea." Liam hesitated, then added, "I have Shauna staying with my cousin Elizabeth Walton while we work the case."

Garrett lifted a brow. "Pretty smart. Doubt the shooter will think to look for her among the Amish."

"That's the goal." He drummed his fingers on the desktop. "But we need something to go on. Shauna claims she has no idea why anyone is after her, and I believe her. David McKay seems equally perplexed by the crime. Given her mother's somewhat checkered past, I can't help but think there might be a revenge angle here."

"Anything is possible," Garrett agreed. "But it sounds like our first task is to identify the dead guy."

"I took pictures of him." Liam used his phone to share them with Garrett. "Let's get these printed out and start talking to the locals and with the area motels. Hopefully someone will remember him."

"Will do." Garrett rose to his feet. "You may want to ask Shauna, too."

"Good point." He nodded. "I'll head back to the Amish Shoppe right away."

Liam headed back outside, stopping when his phone rang again. He was surprised to note the call was from the medical examiner. "Do you have something already?"

"I'm not sure how helpful this will be, but there are imprints along your victim's back, indicating he was lying on pine needles. Like a bed of them."

Green Lake County covered 380 square miles, and a quarter of that was wooded. The rest was used for farming, primarily by the Amish. But taking into consideration the location where the body had been pulled from the water, he thought the scene of the murder might be a little north. There was a large wooded section there. "Thanks, Doc. I'll see what I can find."

Rather than heading straight to the Amish Shoppe, he detoured to the location he had in mind. A large patch of pine trees not far off one of the rural highways. The victim didn't have the physical build of someone who liked to hike, which made Liam think he must have been in a vehicle at some point prior to the murder.

As he approached the group of pine trees, he looked for an abandoned vehicle. There wasn't one in the area, but he decided to check the woods out anyway. Clouds occasionally darkened the sky, so he grabbed his flashlight before getting out of the sedan.

It didn't take him long to find the crime scene. Even without the flashlight, he could see the dark bloodstains soaking the pine needle–covered ground. He called Garrett to let him know what he'd found, then proceeded to take photographs with his phone.

The victim's car was likely stashed somewhere nearby, unless the killer had taken it with him. Had the dead man been transported to the lake in the trunk of his own vehicle? Highly likely.

Liam hiked out of the woods to scan the ground, searching for tire marks. He didn't find any, which made him think the victim had been lured into the woods.

Or forced there at gunpoint.

Only after his deputies arrived and they'd secured the crime scene did he head back to the Amish Shoppe. On the way he called the medical examiner to let him know they'd likely found the crime scene. "I'll need you to match the blood I found with the victim to know for sure."

"Send me a sample—happy to have it tested. A full DNA analysis will take a while, but I can tell you if it's the same blood type as the victim."

"I'll take whatever evidence I can get," Liam assured him. "Garrett will send you the sample. Thanks."

As he pulled into the parking lot, his stomach rumbled with hunger. It was lunchtime, and his breakfast with Shauna seemed like eons ago.

The Amish Shoppe had a small restaurant, similar to Rachel Miller's café. He'd gladly treat Shauna to lunch—if the photo of the dead guy didn't ruin her appetite.

He strode into the building, glad to see the place was full of customers. He knew Elizabeth and David counted on tourism to hold them through the long winters. Once the holidays had passed, the storekeepers shortened their hours to three days a week, Thursday through Saturday, and even then, tourism was scarce.

He found Shauna, Elizabeth and David sitting at a small table outside the restaurant. He stood in line to order his food, and when it was ready, he walked over to sit in the empty chair beside Shauna.

"Hey, how are things going?" Shauna asked.

"I have a few questions, but they can wait until we're finished eating." He took a spoonful of the butternut squash soup. It was as great as he remembered. "How was your morning?"

"Shauna sold a cradle for me," David said.

"And a quilt for me," Elizabeth added. "She's talented with marketing, ain't so?"

"Very much," David agreed. He finished his meal and eyed Liam thoughtfully. "No leads on Shauna's case?"

He shrugged and continued eating. After Shauna, David and Elizabeth were finished with their food, he pulled out his cell phone and swiped the screen until he found the picture of his victim. He set the phone between Shauna and David. "I know this may be a disturbing image, but I need to know if you recognize this man." Shauna gasped and put a hand over her mouth. He straightened in his seat. "You know him?"

"J-Jeff Clancy." Her voice was barely a whisper. "What happened? Why was he here?"

"I was hoping you could tell me." Placing a hand on Shauna's arm, he could feel her body trembling. "How do you know him? Is he a boyfriend?"

"No. A classmate." She pulled her gaze from the photograph. "We were leaving class together when my mom called. She told me to get out of town, to find Uncle Davy, but then I heard a cry and the phone went dead. Jeff came with me to her trailer, and he saw her dead body, too."

He longed to pull Shauna into his arms. Scooting his chair closer to hers, he put a reassuring arm around her shoulders. "Okay, so he was at the trailer with you. Then what happened?"

"I—I left him there. He called 911 to report what we'd found, but I took off and left him there." She buried her face in her hands. "It's my fault he's dead," she murmured.

"You didn't kill him, Shauna. Someone else did. Probably the same person who killed your mother and ran you off the road." He glanced at David, who looked just as sick to his stomach. "I'm sorry to bring bad news."

"'Tis your job, *ja*?" Elizabeth's face had turned pale beneath her *kapp*.

"It is my fault." Shauna's voice was stronger now. She lifted her head and swiped at her face. "I left him there without a car! To deal with my mother's death, just so I could save myself!"

"No, Shauna, you can't think about it like that," David said gently. "An evil person killed your mother and tried to kill you. I suspect Jeff came here specifically to find you—maybe to offer his support, don't you think?"

Shauna sniffled and frowned. "How did he know where to find me? I know he was standing next to me when my mom told me to go to Uncle David to keep me safe, but how did he know Davy lived in Green Lake?"

"He could have looked up the address for David McKay, although I'm sure there's more than one person with that name." Liam considered her point. "Or he managed to follow you."

"His car was at the community college, so I'm not sure how he could have," Shauna insisted. Then she jumped up. "Excuse me. I need to find the restroom." She hurried away.

"Do you think it's possible the killer lured Clancy here?" David asked. "Although, I'm not sure why he would do such a thing."

"I don't know." It made sense that Clancy had been silenced because he was at the trailer with Shauna, before the bad guys had gotten a chance to plant the drugs. And the killer might have assumed Shauna had confided in him. Yet why wait until Green Lake to do that?

Liam had to admit that finding his victim's identity hadn't solved anything. Instead, he had more questions than answers.

Along with a very bad feeling that whoever this killer was, he had access to information that the average person didn't.

Like someone within law enforcement, or someone with deep pockets.

Either option wasn't remotely reassuring.

SEVEN

Hiding in the bathroom stall, Shauna swallowed hard, pressing a hand to her stomach to avoid throwing up her lunch. Her friend was dead, and no matter what Liam or Davy said, it was her fault.

She shouldn't have let Jeff accompany her to her mother's trailer. If he'd stayed behind, she knew he'd still be alive.

Yet the entire situation still didn't make sense. Why had Jeff been targeted? Just because he'd been at her mother's crime scene? He'd called 911, and she'd just left him there.

Left him to handle the mess.

I'm sorry, Jeff. I'm so sorry.

Tears streamed down her cheeks. She'd cried more in the past two days than she had in her entire life.

Including the times her mother had been arrested and the day she'd learned about Eric's lies. That he was married with kids.

It took her a few minutes to get herself under control. She finally splashed cold water on her face, avoiding the stitches but getting the edges of her white *kapp* damp in the process. She still wasn't accustomed to wearing it. She stared at her reflection and told herself to get back out there. The best thing she could do for Jeff now was to help Liam find his killer.

How? She had no clue. But leaving town was no longer an option. Not if Jeff's killer was still here in Green Lake. Jeff didn't deserve to be murdered.

And neither had her mother.

"Shauna?" Davy was waiting for her outside the restrooms. "Are you okay?"

"I will be." She forced a smile and tried to stem the disappointment that Liam wasn't there. "We should get back to the store."

"Yes, but Liam wanted me to let you know that he had to leave. A deputy found an abandoned car they believe belonged to your friend."

"He drove a red Prius," she murmured. Something she should have told Liam before he left.

"I'm sure Liam will verify that," Davy assured her. "Come, let's go back to the store. You can rest in the back for a bit."

"I don't need to rest." She lifted her chin. "Staying busy would be better."

Davy nodded and escorted her through the Amish barn to his furniture store. But her goal to stay busy was futile. Oh, there were plenty of customers, but they were lookers, not buyers.

"Don't worry, Shauna," Davy assured her. "Sometimes they come back another day to buy. Some of my furniture is expensive, so people don't buy willy-nilly."

She wanted to ask how he supported himself with these low sales but held her tongue. For one thing, he didn't have much in the way of expenses. No cell phone, no car, no cable TV.

Maybe there was something to be said for living the simple life.

She tugged at her dress and apron. As much as she wasn't used to them, Elizabeth's generous offer was appreciated. And, really, the fabric was rather comfortable.

About thirty minutes before closing, she wondered how she and Elizabeth would get back to her house. Would Liam return to give them a ride? She scanned the barn, searching for him, when she saw a familiar-looking man abruptly turn away.

Who was he? How did she know him?

"Something wrong?" Davy asked.

Shauna's heart thudded heavily in her chest. "That guy looked familiar," she said in a low voice, trying to place where she'd seen him before.

Davy stepped around so that he was keeping her hidden behind his larger frame. "Do you think he's the driver of the black pickup truck?"

"I—don't know." She gripped Davy's arm. "Get Elizabeth. We need to hide until he's gone."

Her uncle hesitated, then nodded. "Good idea."

They didn't waste any time. Davy helped Elizabeth lock up her store. Then they hurried through the showroom into Davy's workroom.

"We need to call Liam," she whispered.

Davy glanced at Elizabeth, then shrugged. "We don't have phones."

Okay, she changed her mind about the simple life. A phone to call the police would be really helpful right now. Liam had been so busy he hadn't had time to get one for her. Elizabeth sat in a wooden rocking chair that hadn't been stained or varnished.

"One of the customers probably has a cell phone," Shauna said. No way could she just sit here doing nothing. "I'll go and ask one of them to call the police."

"Wait. Are you sure that man looked familiar?" Davy came to stand beside her.

"I only saw him for a moment, but I know I've seen him before. I just can't remember where."

"What did he look like?"

She took a deep breath, trying to think back. "Wiry build, longish blond hair hanging over his forehead…" She snapped her fingers. "That's it—I remember now. He looked like a guy I've seen hanging around on campus."

"A college student?" Davy's brow creased in a frown.

"I—think so. He usually carried a textbook under his arm. Although, now that I think about it, it's odd that he didn't have a backpack like most of us students. I mean, most students usually take notes, either handwritten or on a computer. A book alone seems strange."

Davy's expression darkened. "Maybe he wasn't really a student."

She stared at her uncle as understanding dawned. "You may be right. Mom claimed she was being followed, but I didn't listen. What if I was being followed, too? That same guy could have followed me all the way to my mother's trailer, then again as I left to come here. He must be the one who rammed into me on the overpass."

"We don't know that for certain, but have faith, Shauna. God is watching over you, and I know Liam will figure it out," Davy assured her.

Shauna really wanted to believe her uncle was right. That she was still alive might be because God was watching over her. But thinking about Jeff Clancy, who'd been murdered just for helping her, she wasn't so sure. She moved past her uncle. "Stay here with Elizabeth. I'm going to find a phone."

Her uncle hesitated. "Best you stay here with Elizabeth. I'll find the phone."

"No, a woman is more likely to loan a phone to another female. Besides, this is my problem, not yours." Shauna turned and hurried to the front of the store. The crowd of customers had thinned out, likely as several shops had already closed for the evening.

Keeping her head down, Shauna hurried toward a family of four, parents and two children. She cast a quick glance around to check for the man with stringy blond hair but didn't see him. She managed a smile. "Excuse me—may I borrow your phone? I—need to make a call."

The couple looked at her oddly. The woman drew her young children closer to her side. "I thought the Amish didn't use phones?"

"We don't own them, but we can use them." It was what Elizabeth and Davy had said about cars, so she figured the same rules applied.

Before either of them could respond, there was a loud crash. Shauna spun around in time to see several broken jars of jams and jellies, along with a man rushing off toward the main entrance.

No! He was getting away!

Shauna bolted after the fake college student. Upon reaching the main entrance, she glanced around wildly, trying to figure out which way he went.

A large black truck roared out of the parking lot. She took off running, hoping to get the license plate, but she was too late.

The truck took a curve in the road and disappeared from view.

Leaving Shauna to stare helplessly after it.

Liam was notified the moment the 911 call came through Dispatch about a suspicious man at the Amish Shoppe. He ran to the closest squad car, turning on the red lights and sirens to get there as quickly as possible.

During the entire drive, all he could think about was Shauna. That the killer had found her. That she was right now in his clutches.

Please, Lord. I know I don't deserve Your grace, but please keep Shauna safe!

Despite his bone-deep exhaustion, his mind was sharp as he swiftly entered the large red barn housing the shops. He raked his gaze over the interior of the Sunshine Café, where they'd had lunch earlier, seeing the display of jellies and jams lying on its side. Several of the glass jars were broken and oozing a gooey mess in bright red raspberry and purple blueberry smears.

A pleasant-faced Amish girl was picking up the jars that weren't broken and placing them in a neat stack. He searched the Amish women nearby but didn't see Shauna or Elizabeth.

"What happened?" he asked, glancing around the café. "Who called 911?"

There was a long moment of silence before a woman in her midfifties rose from her seat at a square table. "Sheriff, a man came barreling out from the restrooms and slammed right into the jam display, knocking everything on the floor. He didn't stop or bother to apologize but ran out of here as if his hair was on fire."

Liam frowned. "You made the call to the sheriff's department?"

"Yes, I did." She crossed plump arms across her chest and met his gaze directly. "I called because the man acted oddly, as if he were trying to hide or something. Then he took off without even bothering to pay for the damage." She looked outraged at the guy's callousness. "The Amish people work hard to make a living. Men like him are a disgrace to society."

"*Ach*, 'tis nothing," the Amish woman said in a soft voice. She didn't meet his gaze directly, out of respect more than disdain, he knew. "A mess can be cleaned, ain't so?"

Liam realized he might have overreacted to the 911 call about a suspicious man, when another woman stepped forward. This time, he recognized Shauna. He longed to pull her into his arms but had to settle for drawing her away from the group. "Are you okay? Did you ask that woman to call 911?"

"I would have, but not because of the mess." Shauna stared grimly up at him. "I followed the man who knocked over the display. He drove off in a large black truck."

Liam frowned. "Why did he leave in a rush?"

"I think he may have noticed me staring at him," she admitted. "I recognized him, Liam. Not by name, but his face. I saw him several times on campus over the past few weeks." Her expression turned somber. "I believe he may have been following me, even before my mother's murder. And if so, it's likely he had something to do with it."

He nodded slowly. It made sense and might be a clue as to the killer's identity. "I need a detailed description of this guy. I'd like you to work with a sketch artist." He glanced around. "Where are David and Elizabeth?"

"We're here," David said, stepping forward. "We came to check on Shauna."

"Sheriff?" The woman who'd called 911 moved closer. "I can give you a description of that man."

"Great." He glanced at Davy. "Take the women to your shop. I'll be there soon."

"But—" Shauna began to protest, then stopped when he gave her an exasperated look.

"Please, Shauna," he murmured. "As soon as I'm finished here, I'll come find you, okay?"

She reluctantly nodded and turned away. He focused his attention on the Good Samaritan. "You saw this man?"

"Yes, I did." She seemed to thrive on reporting this crime. "He was tall, but not as tall as you, Sheriff. Maybe five-ten or five-eleven. He was a lean, wiry guy wearing black jeans and a black hoodie sweatshirt. He had long, stringy blond hair that hung low on his forehead." She scowled. "I only caught a glimpse of his face, but he had suspicious eyes."

"Suspicious eyes?" he echoed. What in the world

did that mean? He forced himself to nod and smile. "That's a very good description—thanks. Do you remember his shoes? Or any other identifying marks? Tattoos or piercings?"

"I didn't see any tattoos or piercings, but I wouldn't be surprised if he had them." She sniffed in derision, having obviously taken an instant dislike to the guy. "I didn't look at his shoes. Sorry."

"You've been very helpful," Liam assured her. "Could I have your name and address, in case I have additional questions?"

"Of course." The woman preened with importance as she provided her name and number. "I hope you catch that man. He's a menace to society."

In more ways than one, Liam thought as he turned away. He crossed over to the Amish girl cleaning up the mess. "Would you like help with that?"

"*Ach,* no. 'Tis fine." The girl didn't meet his gaze.

"Could I have your name, please? If I find this man, I'll make him pay for the damages."

The offer of repayment caused the girl to look up at him. "My name is Leah Moore, and I'd be right grateful to recover some of the damage."

"Thanks for telling me. Once I have him in custody, I'll make sure you get reimbursed."

She nodded and turned back to her task. Liam blew out a breath and strode down the center aisle until he reached David's furniture store.

Shauna's uncle unlocked the door and gestured for him to come inside. He brushed past and found Shauna and Elizabeth seated at a small table.

"I'll give you a ride home." His tone did not invite argument. "Stay here, and I'll drive around back."

"I'll watch over them," David promised.

"Thanks." Less than three minutes later, Liam drove his squad car to the rear doorway of David's workshop. He stood for a moment, scanning the area, but didn't see any sign of a black truck or a man with stringy blond hair.

Shauna opened the door to his knock. "We're ready," she said. "I need you to convince Davy to stay with us."

"It wouldn't be proper," David said firmly. "There's no reason to upset Elizabeth's mother-in-law. Besides, I'm not the one in danger."

"You can stay with me in my guest room," Liam offered. "I don't mind."

"I'll be fine," David repeated. "I can bunk here in my workroom. No one will think to look for me here."

"We don't know that for sure," Shauna pointed out. "We don't have any idea why my mother was killed in the first place, much less why I'm still being targeted by this guy."

"I have a theory," Davy said.

She swung around to stare at her uncle. "You do?"

Davy grimaced and spread his hands. "It's just a theory. I don't know anything for sure—no proof to back it up."

"What kind of theory?" Liam stared at David, hoping Shauna's uncle wasn't holding back on him, too. He needed all the cooperation he could get to get this guy off the street.

"Linda—Shauna's mother—often talked about

getting what she deserved from Shauna's father." Davy's tone was grim.

Shauna frowned. "I asked about my father, but Mom claimed she didn't know who he was."

Davy nodded. "Yes, that much is true. But I think there are—were—several possibilities. Linda asked me for help in tracking them down, but I told her there was no point in digging up the past. At twenty-three, almost twenty-four, you're an adult, Shauna. It's not like Linda could get child support or any sort of income from your biological father at this late date."

Liam frowned as Shauna sank into the closest chair. If she looked pale before, her skin was ashen now. He edged closer, ready to grab her if she toppled over.

"That doesn't make any sense," she whispered mostly to herself. "I don't get it. Why would Mom try to find my biological father after all these years? Why would it matter?"

"I don't know," David admitted.

"How long ago did you talk to Linda about that?" Liam asked.

David looked thoughtful. "As I said, I haven't spoken to her in the past two years. She seemed determined to find Shauna's father and wasn't happy when I refused to help."

"She's been trying to find my father all this time?" Shauna asked. "Then why on earth would someone try to come after her now?"

Liam had to admit that David's theory didn't seem relevant. "I agree. It's unlikely that an attempt to find Shauna's biological father would cause this drastic chain of events. Premeditated murder of not just Linda but Jeff Clancy? Attempted murder of Shauna? Because of a liaison that took place twenty-four years ago? I'm not seeing it."

Davy looked uncomfortable for a moment. "My sister was only sixteen when she became pregnant with Shauna. At the time she—uh—worked in a strip club using a fake ID. She only did it to help put food on the table. Our mother was—in rough shape at the time."

"What?" Shauna swayed as if physically struck by the news. Liam quickly wrapped his arm around her shoulders. "Why didn't she tell me?"

"I'm sorry," David said softly. "But Linda asked me to keep the truth a secret from you."

"I knew she was young when she had me, but…" Shauna's voice trailed off. Liam felt bad she was learning the truth now.

"I—need a moment." Shauna abruptly stood and ducked outside. This time, Liam quickly followed.

"Shauna, none of this is your fault."

"Yeah? Then why does it feel like it is?" Her voice was full of agony. "I was so impatient with my mother, especially with her substance abuse issues. I didn't treat her with as much compassion as I should have, and now it's too late…" She buried her face in her hands.

This time, Liam couldn't stop himself from gathering her into his arms. "Shh, it's not your fault."

Shauna leaned into his embrace, gripping his jacket with her hands. "If I could go back in time, I'd do things differently."

"Me, too." Hadn't he gone through this same emotional roller coaster after Jerica and Mikey had died? "I lost my wife and son because of a rift in our marriage. Because I'd turned a blind eye to the troubles we were having. She was so unhappy with me that she found another man. After they died, it was too late to fix things."

Shauna lifted her head to gaze up at him. "You know how this feels."

"I do." He tucked a strand of her dark hair into her *kapp*. "My relationship with God has been rocky, but over time, I've come to accept that it's not my place to question God's plan. He has provided this life for us, and our job is to live in His honor."

"How do you deal with the guilt?"

"I'm still learning," he admitted. Although, since Shauna had come into his life, he'd thought of Jerica and Mikey less than usual. "We can't go back, Shauna. No matter how much we wish we could."

"I guess I'll learn to live with the guilt, too," she whispered. "Thank you, Liam." She stood on her tiptoes and kissed him.

All rational thought evaporated as their lips meshed, clung, held. He gathered her closer and kissed her the way he hadn't kissed any woman in well over two years.

Wishing he never had to stop.

EIGHT

Losing herself in Liam's warm embrace was wonderful, but the sound of a door opening had her abruptly breaking off their kiss, stepping backward so fast she almost lost her balance.

"Everything okay?" Davy asked.

"We're fine." Shauna fought the urge to cover her heated cheeks with her hands. "We should go."

"I'll get Elizabeth." Davy turned back inside.

She stared at the ground, her mind whirling. She'd kissed Liam! What was she thinking? This was hardly the time or the place to start anything.

"I'm sorry," she began, then stopped when Davy and Elizabeth stepped out of the Amish barn. Her uncle closed and locked the door before coming over to join them.

"I'm not," Liam said as he opened the rear passenger door of his squad car. "David, you and Elizabeth should get in the back. I'll bring you back to the Amish Shoppe after we drop the women off."

"'Tis a new experience for me, riding in a police car," Elizabeth murmured.

David didn't respond to Elizabeth, his gaze seemingly locked on Shauna instead. She felt sure that he knew she'd kissed Liam.

Honestly, she needed to get a grip on her rioting emotions. One minute she was devastated over learning the truth about her mother's checkered past, the next she was throwing herself at a man.

That he wasn't sorry about their kiss stayed with her as she slid into the passenger seat. He'd lost his wife and son, his wife cheating on him with another man, but he wasn't sorry she'd kissed him.

What did that mean? He'd welcome another kiss?

No, don't go there, she warned. Didn't she have enough problems at the moment? Someone was trying to kill her. Adding another complication would push her over the edge.

The trip to Elizabeth's house didn't take too long, although she noticed the community where Elizabeth lived was outside the city limits, closer to Dalton than Green Lake. The farms were spread out over many acres of land, although it appeared the harvest was completed by now.

Several Amish girls were walking along the road, and she recognized them from the Sunshine Café. They eyed the police vehicle warily as Liam drove by.

When Liam stopped the car in front of Elizabeth's house, Shauna swallowed a wave of apprehension. Their earlier visit had been quick, but now she'd be spending the night.

Davy offered his hand to help Elizabeth out of the back seat. *"Denke,"* she murmured in a low voice.

"You're welcome," Davy responded. "I look forward to seeing you tomorrow, Elizabeth."

"Certain sure," she replied before turning toward Shauna. "*Komm*, we'll get you settled, *ja*?"

"Yes, thank you. Good night, Liam. See you tomorrow, Davy." Shauna didn't let her gaze linger on Liam as she joined Elizabeth, and she had to fight the urge to beg Davy to take her with him. Then remembered he was bunking in his workroom.

"*Wilkom* to my home, Shauna," Elizabeth said as they stepped into the kitchen.

"It's very nice." When they'd come earlier to get the clothing, she hadn't taken much time to look around. Now she was curious. The atmosphere was cozy and warm despite the austere furniture. Pale green curtains and darker green kitchen towels were hand sewn, just like the quilts Elizabeth sold at her shop.

How long did it take to make a quilt by hand? Shauna wondered. She couldn't begin to imagine.

"Are you hungry? I have bread and soup left from last evening's supper."

"That would be nice, thank you." Shauna took a seat at the kitchen table as Elizabeth set about warming up the soup. When that was finished, she filled a bowl and set it on a tray for her mother-in-law.

"*Mammi* Ruth prefers to eat in her room. I'll return shortly, *ja*?"

"I understand."

After the elder woman had been provided for, Elizabeth set another bowl before Shauna, along with a thick slice of homemade bread. Shauna accepted the simple fare, bowing her head as Elizabeth said grace, before taking a tentative bite. The food was wonderful, making her realize how hungry she'd been.

"Elizabeth, is there something you need me to do for your mother-in-law yet tonight?"

"*Ach*, no, tomorrow morning will be soon enough," Elizabeth assured her. "*Mammi* Ruth doesn't even know you're here yet. I'll fill her in later. For now, you need to get some rest. We rise early, ain't so?"

"That's not a problem," Shauna assured her. She finished the meal and then insisted on washing and drying the dishes so Elizabeth could care for her mother-in-law, determined not to cause the sweet Amish woman any trouble.

When they were finished with their respective tasks, Elizabeth showed her to her room. Summoning a smile, she turned to her hostess. "Thank you for everything, Elizabeth. I'm very thankful for how you've welcomed me into your home."

"*Ach*, 'tis no trouble. I'm looking forward to having another woman to talk to. See you in the morning, Shauna."

She hadn't expected to sleep—or, at least, not very well, considering her strange surroundings—but the next thing she knew, it was morning, the sun barely peeking over the horizon.

The morning hours passed quickly. Shauna helped Elizabeth by cleaning the kitchen while she cared for *Mammi* Ruth. Overhearing part of the conversation—at least, the parts she could understand amid the Pennsylvania Dutch—Shauna understood Elizabeth's mother-in-law to be a bit cantankerous.

Working side by side with Elizabeth gave Shauna a

new appreciation for the Amish people. Not only did they work hard, but they did what needed to be done without a single complaint. As they got ready to leave, Elizabeth bundled a large sewing bag. "I'm making another wedding quilt," she explained. "They are big sellers, along with the baby quilts."

"I can't wait to see it," Shauna said with a smile.

A horse-drawn buggy showed up outside Elizabeth's home. Shauna was introduced to one of the Amish elders, a man by the name of Ezekiel Moore. Surprisingly, Shauna enjoyed the ride, although she doubted it would be as nice in the frigid winter months.

"Does Mr. Moore always give you a ride to the Amish barn?" Shauna asked.

"'Tis the way our community supports one another, *ja*?" Elizabeth explained. "After my husband passed away, the men in our community have offered their assistance in one way or another."

Shauna wondered if this was a way for Ezekiel Moore to court Elizabeth, hoping to marry her, but she didn't ask. After the elder Amish man helped them from the buggy, they approached the main entrance to the Amish Shoppe. Shauna's stomach churned with concern as she wondered if the blond-haired man would show up again today.

Looking for her.

Maybe she should ask Liam about the disposable phone, although there wouldn't be a place to plug it in to charge it at Elizabeth's house. Yet she didn't like not having something to use if they experienced another emergency. Elizabeth stood outside the door for a moment, glancing back to the road.

"Is there a problem?" Shauna asked. Mr. Moore was already driving the buggy away.

"*Ach*, no. The others will be here shortly."

Soon a group of Amish women came on foot, the same group they'd passed walking home last evening. Apparently, Elizabeth was their unspoken leader.

The way they greeted each other made Shauna realize how closely the Amish were bonded, especially the women. Elizabeth introduced her, and the women regarded her with open curiosity but no sign of malice.

She was humbled by their easy acceptance of her, despite being an *Englisch* outsider.

They had barely gotten settled in their respective shops, with Elizabeth working on her quilt while Shauna manned Davy's showroom, when Liam arrived. He looked so handsome, so self-assured in his casual clothing—no uniform this time—that she felt embarrassed all over again about how she'd kissed him.

"Do you have time to work with a sketch artist?" Liam glanced from her to Davy. "I hope to provide my deputies the likeness of the blond-haired man as they patrol the area."

"I've never done that before, but I'm willing to try." She forced a smile. "If Davy can manage without me for a while."

"I've been doing this alone for years," Davy assured her. "I'll be fine."

"Stay here. I'll come around back again," Liam instructed. "Best not to have you seen with me walking through the shopping area."

"Okay." Ten minutes later, she met Liam behind the

Amish barn. "Can I remove my *kapp* for a bit?" She glanced at him. "It's probably more noticeable for me to have it on while riding with you."

"Of course." He lifted a brow. "How was your night without creature comforts?"

"It was fine—better than I'd expected." She smiled wryly as she patted her bound hair. Elizabeth had helped pull her long hair back, wrapping it in a tight bun to be covered by the *kapp*. "Reminded me of living in my mother's trailer that first year, when we didn't always have money to pay the electric bill."

"Sounds like those were difficult times."

She shrugged. Back then, she'd been angry with her mother for drinking their money away, but after learning about the circumstances around her birth, she wished she'd been more supportive. "Everyone has difficulties. Mine aren't unique."

"Some worse than others," Liam insisted. "You've risen above your past, Shauna. That's something to be proud of."

After the horrible way she'd treated her mother? Not happening.

"You and Jeff Clancy weren't dating?"

Liam's question came out of left field. "No. Why would you ask that? I told you we were just friends."

"You're a beautiful woman, Shauna. I guess I'm trying to understand why you don't have a man in your life."

"Because the one guy I dated for nearly a year was already married with two children, a fact he neglected to mention." She twisted the *kapp* with her fingers, wishing she hadn't been so gullible. "The whole thing soured me on dating. Besides, I don't need a man to be happy."

"No, you don't. But trust me when I say living your life alone isn't fun, either."

"I'm sorry for your loss, Liam." She couldn't imagine any woman leaving him for another man, but she didn't have time to say anything more as he pulled up to the police station.

The interior was fairly empty—she imagined the deputies were out on patrol. There was one man standing there, dressed in uniform, next to a woman with short blond hair.

"Shauna, this is Deputy Garrett Nichol and sketch artist Jacy Urban."

"Nice to meet you," Shauna said with a nod.

"This way," Garrett said, leading Shauna and Jacy to an empty desk.

Shauna was nervous about the process, but Jacy walked her through it. It took longer than she'd anticipated, but when they were finished, Jacy gestured to the final product. "What do you think? Anything else we need to tweak?"

"That's him," Shauna said, staring at the man she'd assumed was a college student. "That's the guy from the Amish Shoppe yesterday."

And, very likely, the man who'd killed her mother. After spending time that morning praying with Elizabeth and listening to a passage from the Bible, Shauna found herself silently praying to God now. She prayed God would give Liam the strength and knowledge he needed to find and arrest this man.

Before he hurt anyone else.

* * *

Sleep hadn't come easily last night, and Liam knew the blame rested on Shauna's kiss.

The one he wasn't sorry about, even if she was.

Hearing about her experience with a man who'd lied to her about being married, he could understand her hesitation. And hadn't he convinced himself that despite how much he'd enjoyed their kiss, it couldn't happen again?

Not just because he was tasked with keeping her safe, but really, he wasn't ready to become emotionally involved again. His marriage had fallen apart, mostly because of his long hours, since being sheriff wasn't a nine-to-five job. His wife had made several trips home to Madison, which he now realized was just her way of seeing another man. Someone who would provide her with everything Liam didn't have.

Looking back, he remembered Elizabeth's warning about how Jerica didn't share his faith. It hadn't seemed like a big deal at first, but over time, Jerica had resented the way he'd attend services, either in town or with the Amish. She claimed he was using that as an excuse to avoid spending time with her.

And maybe there was a kernel of truth to that. Attending church had brought a sense of peace. Something he'd craved because Jerica was so unhappy.

"Sheriff?" Jacy approached with the sketch. "Here's your guy."

Casting his gaze over the drawing, he nodded. The detail was excellent. "Thanks, Jacy. Great work."

"Your witness was really good." Jacy turned, then hesitated, glancing back at him. "Is she in danger?"

He didn't discuss active cases, but he slowly nodded. "Yeah. Be careful on your way back to Fond du Lac."

"Will do." Jacy turned and left.

"I'll get copies of this out to the deputies," Garrett offered. "If he's skulking around town, we'll find him."

"Thanks. I may go back to the Amish Shoppe, in case he shows up there again." Liam didn't like the way the guy had taken off running after Shauna recognized him.

His phone rang, and he straightened in his seat when he recognized the medical examiner. He gestured for Garrett to stay and put the phone on speaker. "Harland."

"Sheriff, I'm calling to let you know I finished my autopsy. I can confirm cause of death is a gunshot wound to the temple, and at close range. There were gunpowder burns around the entry site."

"Any estimate on time of death?" Liam asked.

"As I thought, twelve hours, give or take a few. Hard to know with how cold the lake is, and after he'd been lying on those pine needles for several hours before he was moved."

Garrett spoke up. "What about the blood sample I sent over? Did you get a chance to match it with our victim?"

"I did. It's the same blood type, and a relatively rare one—type O negative. Only fifteen percent of the population has negative blood, so I'm inclined to believe you found the murder site. However, we'll need to do a DNA match on both blood samples to say for sure."

Liam noticed Shauna was hovering outside the

doorway, listening in. He quickly took the call off speaker and lifted the phone to his ear. "Thanks, Doc. Keep me posted on anything else you find."

"Of course. Take care, Sheriff."

Garrett scowled at Shauna. "This is official business."

"Yeah, business that includes me," she shot back. "It was my friend and my mother that were both murdered. I have a right to know what's going on."

Liam admired her spunk, and her loyalty to her friend. "It's fine, Garrett. Why don't you get that sketch scanned into the computer and sent out to the deputies?"

His chief deputy nodded, rose to his feet and left. Liam eyed Shauna. "You did a great job with the sketch. You have a good eye for detail."

"Thanks." She paused, then added, "Did Jeff really die the previous night, rather than yesterday morning?"

"He did. And we found his vehicle, too. A red Prius. There was a GPS system in the car, so he must have overheard you saying something about Green Lake, as that destination was programmed in."

Shauna frowned. "I didn't say Green Lake, but my mom did. Maybe Jeff was able to hear part of my mother's conversation while I was talking to her."

"Makes sense," he agreed.

"He was coming to help me, even after I left him behind." Shauna's voice was full of self-reproach. "Only to die for his efforts."

"Not by your hand, Shauna." He knew what it was like to live with guilt. "Thanks to your sketch, we'll find the blond dude."

Her gaze was skeptical, but she nodded. "Thanks for telling me about Jeff."

"You're welcome." He stood. "I'd better get you back to the Amish Shoppe." Since she was staying with Elizabeth without access to electricity, he'd decided against buying her a phone. It would be impossible to keep it charged up and ready to go.

Shauna didn't say much as he drove her back. He could tell she was ruminating on the details surrounding Jeff's murder.

He escorted Shauna around back so she could enter the store through David's workroom. Most of the customers in the Amish Shoppe were tourists, and other than David, all the shop owners were Amish, but it didn't hurt to be extra cautious.

Liam drove around to the front of the building and sat for a few minutes to look for the blond guy. The sketch was imprinted on his mind, but he didn't see any sign of him. As much as he wanted to stay and keep an eye on Shauna, he forced himself to patrol the town and surrounding rural areas of Green Lake, doing his part to identify their suspect.

The hours went by with agonizing slowness. He was frustrated with the lack of progress on the case. When he drove past the motel where he'd taken Shauna that first night, he decided to stop in and talk to the clerk.

"Have you seen this man?" He showed the clerk, Cliff, a copy of Shauna's sketch.

"Maybe," Cliff agreed, scratching his whiskers. The man looked to be in his late sixties. "He kinda looks like the guy who stayed in room three last night."

Liam's pulse quickened. Last night? "Is he still there?"

"Not sure. Checkout time is eleven, but I don't think the maid has gone into that room yet." Cliff grinned. "Betty is my wife of forty years. She wouldn't be happy to be referred to as a maid."

"I'm Sheriff Harland, and I need to see that room right away." He prayed Betty hadn't gotten around to cleaning it.

"Sure." Cliff grabbed a key card and came around the counter. Outside, Liam could see a cleaning cart parked between rooms three and four.

"Cliff, didn't you tell that guy checkout time is eleven?" Betty demanded, her hands planted on plump hips. "His Do Not Disturb sign is still out."

"Of course I did," Cliff huffed. "What, ya think I don't know the rules?"

"Hold on. Give me that key." Liam took the card from Cliff's hand. "You and Betty need to go into the office. If this man is still in there, he could be armed and dangerous."

"Oh, my stars," Betty murmured as Cliff hustled her out of harm's way.

Liam used his phone to call Garrett. "I need backup. Suspect might be here at the Woodland Escape Motel, five miles outside town."

"Be there in five," Garrett promised.

His deputy arrived in three, and they each took up a position on either side of door number three. Liam knocked and shouted, "Police! Open up!"

No response.

He and Garrett looked at each other. Liam knocked

again and repeated the demand. When there was still no response, he used the key card to unlock the door, then pushed it open with his foot, expecting to be greeted by gunfire.

There was nothing but silence.

"Cover me," Liam said before pushing the door the rest of the way open and entering the room.

It was empty—no sign of any personal belongings having been left behind. Yet the room had clearly been used; the bedsheets were in disarray, and he found wet towels on the floor.

"Look at this." Liam pointed to the smear of red on the towels.

"Too light in color to be blood," Garrett said with a frown. He sniffed. "Doesn't smell like blood, either. It's fruity."

"Yeah, I think it's raspberry jam from when he hit the jelly display yesterday." He slowly rose to his feet. "We need the crime scene techs here. I want them to dust every surface for fingerprints. If this guy has a criminal record, his name will pop in the system. At least then we'll have a name to go with the face."

"On it," Garrett said, moving out of the room to make the call.

Liam stood for a moment, annoyed with himself for not coming here earlier.

Their killer was still on the loose.

NINE

As Shauna chatted with customers browsing in Uncle Davy's shop, she kept a keen eye out for the blond-haired man. She felt certain he'd show up again today, and this time, she planned to be ready.

Unnerving to think back to the various encounters she'd had with him on campus. Not that he'd gotten close, but she did remember one time he'd looked as if he might approach, only to turn away when Jeff had joined her.

Now Jeff was dead. And the fake college student was here in Green Lake.

If he showed up today, she would make sure he didn't get away.

"I have another cradle finished," Davy said, emerging from the workroom. He set the cradle near the front of the store, then stepped back.

For some reason, his cradles made her long for something she'd never planned to have.

A family of her own.

"Great!" She gestured toward Elizabeth's quilt shop. "I'll get another baby quilt, too. That really worked to draw customers in the other day."

"I'm blessed and grateful for any and all sales," Davy agreed. "The winter months tend to be lean."

Now she was worried about him. "Is there anything else I can do to help?"

"No, you're doing more than enough," Davy assured her. "And I stock up on furniture over the winter so that I'm ready to sell come spring."

His practical strategy made her feel slightly better.

"I have some money saved," she offered. "I can't access those funds now—at least, Liam didn't want me to—but once this is over, I'm happy to pay my fair share. Especially since you and Elizabeth are feeding me on top of helping to hide me from the killer."

"Shauna, your company is more than enough. I wish we would have made more time to be together before..." His voice trailed off.

Before her mother was murdered.

"I know." Shauna forced a smile. "I wish I could go back to her trailer, maybe pick up a few personal items. Especially now that everything in my apartment is burned to a crisp."

Davy's eyes suddenly widened. "I totally forgot! I have some of Linda's things. She asked me to store two boxes for her after she moved to the trailer. They're still sitting in my basement." He stared at her. "I wonder if there's something in those boxes that may be helpful to us finding the identity of your biological father."

"That seems a stretch, considering she claims she didn't know who he was." Shauna brightened. "But I would still like to look through her things. Maybe there's a photograph of us tucked away in there."

"She didn't know who your father was, Shauna, but I think she knew who the potential fathers were," Davy corrected softly. "There's a big difference."

Her stomach knotted at the thought of her mother being with more than one man in a short period of time. Guilt assailed her once again. Liam had told her to focus on God's path, but it wasn't easy.

Still, she did her best to let it go. "It's a good idea to check those boxes, Davy. Maybe we will find something useful. When we see Liam, we can ask him to bring them here."

He considered this and nodded. "Okay, that would work."

Once again, she wished she had a phone. Of all the technology she'd given up, that was the one convenience she missed the most.

The hours went by a little faster today, maybe because it was Friday and there were more customers shopping. It made sense that the weekend would be busier than during the week.

Unfortunately, she didn't see any sign of the blond guy. In her mind, that wasn't a good sign. He could be waiting somewhere outside for them to leave.

Twice she took a break to stroll down the center aisle. She was glad to see the display of jams and jellies had been rebuilt, albeit with slightly fewer jars.

The Amish girl gave Shauna a nod of recognition. It didn't take long for her to remember her name was Leah. If Shauna had money, she'd buy some of the woman's jam as a way to offer support. And because the jelly looked delicious.

Yet there was no sign of the blond guy. Shauna

felt certain he was still in the Green Lake area. Had her sketch helped the police? She had to believe Liam would let her know if they'd arrested the guy.

He'd want her to identify him, wouldn't he?

She found herself praying Liam and his deputies would get him in custody very soon. She wanted this nightmare to end.

Not that she had much of a life in Chicago to go back to. The thought was depressing.

The rest of the afternoon went by with only one more sale—not the cradle this time, but a boxy dresser. The couple who purchased it had bought the bed frame a few months ago and now wanted the matching dresser.

"A good day for me," Davy said with a smile when she told him about the sale.

"I'm glad." Shauna was pleased to have been a part of helping him man the store so he could work.

Elizabeth came over, smiling shyly at Davy. "*Sehr gut* news on the sale, *ja*?"

"Very much," Davy agreed.

Shauna couldn't help but wonder about their friendship. David didn't seem inclined to take things further, but then again, maybe Elizabeth wasn't allowed to spend time with men who weren't Amish. Maybe she could ask the woman about that, later that evening.

"Shauna, I need to finish up a few things in my shop. Would you mind escorting these women out front?" Elizabeth asked. "Based on the man ruining Leah's display yesterday, we decided to stay together as much as possible as we walk home. It would be safer for all, certain sure."

Shauna belatedly realized several of the Amish women had gathered near the front entrance to Elizabeth's quilt shop. They were the same group she'd seen several times now, so she nodded.

"Of course." She joined the other women, and together they made their way down the center aisle. The shops were closed, but there were customers milling about, taking their time in leaving the Amish Shoppe.

A rough, bulky man with dark hair and a beard rudely pushed between her and Leah. Shauna heard a loud cry seconds before Leah stumbled and fell to the ground.

"What happened?" Shauna dropped beside her. "Did he hit you?"

"Hurts," Leah whimpered.

"Where?" Then she saw it—a bright red bloodstain growing larger and larger on Leah's white apron.

No! Shauna quickly balled up the other end of the apron and held it against the wound, applying pressure to stop the bleeding. As she looked into Leah's blue eyes, she saw the fear and pain reflected there.

The poor girl had been stabbed, and she instantly knew it was her fault. Not only were they dressed alike, but Leah also had dark hair. Granted, Leah didn't have stitches on her forehead, but maybe the guy hadn't been paying close enough attention. Either way, there wasn't a doubt in Shauna's mind that she was the intended target, not Leah.

A wave of guilt hit hard. Another innocent person had been hurt because someone was intent on killing her.

How many more would suffer because of her?

* * *

Hovering over the crime scene techs at the motel didn't make them work faster, but Liam hadn't been able to help himself. And the minute they'd lifted several useful prints, he rushed back to the station to get them uploaded into AFIS.

Staring at the screen, he smiled with grim satisfaction as a name and mug shot popped up. The perp's name was Karl Maxwell, and his picture was an uncanny likeness to Shauna's sketch.

His gut told him this was their guy, but he followed their normal procedure of putting Maxwell's mug shot in a photo array with five other guys who looked somewhat similar. He'd present the six-pack of faces to Shauna to see if she could identify Maxwell.

It was their first lead, and he was glad to have it. Although, so far none of his deputies had eyeballed Maxwell. One of the problems was that Green Lake covered so much acreage that finding one guy was like finding a penny lost along a two-mile sandy beach.

Before he could head over to the Amish Shoppe, though, he took a moment to send Maxwell's mug shot to his deputies. Having a name and a real photograph might help them find additional witnesses.

As he was heading to his SUV, one of his deputies called. "A waitress at the diner recognized Shauna's sketch, but she said the guy paid in cash. I just took Maxwell's mug shot over, and she offered a positive ID."

"Good work, Rawson." His deputies had been shocked at the news of Clancy's murder, since that sort of thing rarely happened in Green Lake. Several of them had offered to work overtime to find their perp, too. "Keep checking around. We found his motel room, which is how we got this mug shot. Maybe he dropped his guard and said something we can use. I'm heading to the Amish Shoppe now to verify Shauna's ID."

"On it, boss." Rawson clicked off.

He decided at the last minute to take a squad car, and the moment he slid behind the wheel, the call came through. "Report of a stabbing at the Amish Shoppe. An Amish female has been injured."

Shauna! Liam hit the gas, adding the red lights and sirens to get through traffic in record time. His heart pounded in his chest, and he silently prayed for Shauna's well-being.

Please, Lord, keep Shauna safe in Your care!

The Ripon Medical Center was roughly fifteen minutes away from the east side of town, but the Amish Shoppe was located farther outside the city. Likely a good thirty minutes away.

He barreled into the parking lot before the ambulance arrived. Jumping from his car, he ran into the refurbished barn.

There was a small group of Amish women huddled around a woman stretched out on the floor. A staggering relief hit hard when he saw Shauna kneeling beside the woman, holding pressure on her abdomen.

Shauna hadn't been stabbed, but another woman. As he dropped beside them, he grimly realized the victim was Leah, the Amish girl who ran the Sunshine Café and who had suffered the damage to her jams and jellies. Leah had dark hair and the same slight build as Shauna.

The grim horror in Shauna's eyes confirmed she

also believed this to be a case of mistaken identity. He took control of the situation while offering a silent prayer for God to heal Leah's wound.

"Was it the same man as yesterday?" he asked.

"No, this man was bigger across the shoulders, taller, and had dark hair and a shortly trimmed beard."

Two EMTs came into the Amish barn. Liam stood and urged the other Amish women to back off to give the EMTs space to work.

"Will Leah go to the hospital?" Shauna asked, coming over to stand beside him.

"This community is a bit more progressive than others, so yes, I think she will. Although, her family will meet her there and stay with her the entire time. They'll also want her to spend as little time in the hospital as possible. They'll be prepared to care for her while she recovers at home."

"You know that man was after me," Shauna said in a low voice.

"I'm afraid you're right." He grimaced as Elizabeth and Davy joined them. "I'm sorry, Elizabeth. I shouldn't have asked for your help with Shauna."

"'Tis not Shauna's fault, ain't so?" Despite her kind words, Elizabeth looked pale and shaken. "I pray Leah's injury isn't too severe."

Liam lightly rested his hand on his cousin's arm. "I've been praying for Leah, too, and will continue to do so. But I hate knowing I brought danger to you and your community."

Elizabeth gave a slight nod. "The Bible teaches us to help those in need. I know strangers are not readily welcomed in some Amish communities, but here we do our best to treat our *Englisch* neighbors with honor and respect."

Liam appreciated her not downplaying the danger. "I can drive Leah's family to the hospital."

"*Ach*, that would be a kind gesture, certain sure," Elizabeth said. *"Denke."*

"Liam, you should know that Davy has a couple of boxes containing my mother's things in his basement," Shauna said. "I know we need to make sure Elizabeth and Leah's family are cared for first, but after that we hoped you'd be willing to pick up those boxes and bring them here so we can go through them." She shrugged. "It's possible we'll find something helpful in there."

"Good idea." He turned to Elizabeth. "Would it be okay if I ask Garrett to drive you home and to get Leah's family to the hospital?"

"Of course," Elizabeth agreed. "You can bring Shauna by later."

Liam hesitated. He didn't want to bring more danger to Elizabeth's doorstep, but he didn't have another option. The only good part of Leah's being stabbed was that the bad guys hadn't been able to distinguish one Amish woman from the other.

But how long would this ruse work? He had no idea. Yet he also wasn't ready to abandon the plan entirely. He nodded slowly. "If we are not there by 8:00 p.m., then don't wait up. I can always have Davy and Shauna stay with me for one night."

"Sehr gut," Elizabeth murmured.

Liam called Garrett, who agreed to head out to drive Elizabeth and the other women home and to then take Leah's family to the hospital. Satisfied that one problem had been taken care of, he remembered the six-pack of mug shots he needed to show Shauna.

He ushered her and David back to the furniture store. "We found the motel where the blond guy was staying and ran his prints through the system."

"You caught him?" Shauna asked.

"Not yet, but I'd like you to see if you can make a positive ID." He held out the photo array. "Do you see the man who knocked over Leah's display?"

"This one." She didn't hesitate as she pointed to Karl Maxwell's mug shot. "I'm still kicking myself that I didn't realize he was following me back in Chicago."

"His name is Karl Maxwell." He glanced between Shauna and David. "Does that name ring a bell?"

"Not to me," David said.

"Me, either," Shauna admitted.

"He was arrested in Chicago on charges that included burglary with a deadly weapon," Liam explained. "That's why his prints are in the system. Unfortunately, he didn't do much time in jail and was paroled well over a year ago."

Shauna frowned. "Doesn't sound like the kind of guy to be carrying some sort of grudge against my mother. And he's not old enough to be my biological father, either."

"I know. You said the guy who stabbed Leah was someone different, which means there's at least two men coming after you."

"Do you believe these two men are hired guns?" David asked. "Paid by someone to kill Shauna?"

He reluctantly nodded. "I can't think of another reason to explain how things have played out. There have been several attempts on Shauna's life, first intended to look like an accident, now a more blatant attack in the middle of the shopping area."

"Not very reassuring," Shauna said on a sigh. "I'm so upset Leah was hurt because of me."

"Because some guy stabbed her with a knife," Liam corrected swiftly. "Come on. Let's head over to David's place. If those boxes your mother left behind have any sort of clue buried inside, we need to find it, sooner rather than later."

"Sounds like a plan." Shauna turned toward David. "It's time you stop staying here overnight, Uncle Davy. I think you should take Liam up on his offer to spend the night at his place."

"I will if you will," David shot back. "At least for tonight."

Shauna hesitated and turned toward him. "Liam, do you think it's better for Elizabeth if I don't stay with her tonight?"

"I do, yes. We can reevaluate the plan tomorrow." Liam waited as David locked up. Then they left through the back door of the workshop.

David gave him directions to his home, which wasn't that far from the Amish Shoppe. After pulling into the driveway, they all got out of the car.

"Looks the way I remember," Shauna said with a wry smile.

"You should know the electric has been shut off, but I have a flashlight right inside the front door and several lanterns as well." David led the way, taking a moment to unlock the door before stepping inside.

There was still a little light filtering in through the windows. Once they went down in the basement, though, they needed the flashlight.

"Take the light, Shauna, so David and I can carry the boxes upstairs."

It didn't take long for them to head back outside to his squad car. He and David set the boxes in the trunk. Liam slammed the lid, then frowned as he noticed movement around the far corner of David's house.

"Get inside the car," he ordered. Then he took off running. He heard more footsteps hitting the earth and knew the guy was sprinting away from him, so he put on a burst of speed to catch up.

The guy was only a few yards ahead. From the back he couldn't identify him, but his slim build and long-ish hair reminded him of Karl Maxwell's mug shot.

The man abruptly stopped and turned. When Liam saw the gun in his hand, he dived to the ground and rolled as gunfire echoed around him.

TEN

The sound of gunfire sent Shauna's heart into her throat. "Liam!" With a flash of anger, she pushed open the passenger door and jumped out.

"Shauna, wait!" Davy grasped her arm. "Liam wouldn't want you to be in danger!"

She glanced at Davy's grim face. "I can't just sit here. What if he's injured?" She tried to shake off his hand, but her uncle's grip tightened.

"Please, Shauna, get back inside the squad car. Liam is a cop—I'm sure he has this under control. What if you distract him and cause more harm than good?"

She hesitated, hating to admit Davy might be right. Still, she didn't get back inside the car. The night was silent now, and she wanted—needed—to believe that meant the danger was over.

At least, for now.

"I wish we had a phone," she murmured.

"Do you know how to use the squad radio?"

Davy's question prompted her to get back into the car. "No, but I'll figure it out."

The various dials were confusing, but she found

the power switch and then lifted the hand piece to her mouth. "Can anyone hear me?"

There was no response at first, so she clicked another button and tried again.

"This is Dispatch. What's your twenty?"

"I don't know what that means, but Sheriff Liam Harland needs backup at…" She glanced back at Davy, who quickly supplied his address. "Shots have been fired. I repeat, shots have been fired!"

"Ten-four. Deputies are on the way."

The dispatcher's calm voice grated on Shauna's nerves, although she was grateful for the response. The seconds ticked by in her head, and just as she was about to get out of the car, she saw a figure coming around the corner of Davy's house.

Liam! The shaft of relief was overwhelming.

Thank You, God!

Liam opened her passenger door. "Are you both okay?"

"I called for backup. They're sending deputies," Shauna said, reaching up to take his hand. "The better question is, are you okay? You're not hurt?"

"I'm fine. His aim was off, but after I hit the dirt, he unfortunately got away." Liam's features were etched with frustration. "I didn't give chase for long because I was worried you were both in danger from a potential accomplice. I couldn't be sure the perp was alone."

"I don't understand how that guy knew where Davy lived," she said, glancing between her uncle and Liam. "Do you think we were followed here?"

"No. I kept an eye on the rearview mirror just to make sure no one followed us," Liam said firmly.

"Strange coincidence that the gunman showed up at the same time we did," Davy murmured.

"Maybe they had your place staked out," Liam said with a frown. "Although, you'd think they'd have made their move while we were inside."

"We weren't inside for long," she pointed out. "Maybe they were hiding off in the woods. It may have taken them a few minutes to get here, only by then we were at the car."

Police sirens screeched, blue and red flashing lights growing brighter as the deputies responded to her call. They'd made decent time, considering her uncle's home was in the middle of nowhere.

"Stay here. I'll be back." Liam shut the door and strode over to meet up with the deputies.

"God was watching over us today," Davy said softly. "I'm grateful Liam wasn't hurt."

"Me, too." She turned in her seat to face her uncle. "You've really taken the Amish life to heart, haven't you?"

He nodded slowly. "Not just the life, but their beliefs, especially in God's grace and mercy." A wry smile tugged at the corner of his mouth. "Probably sounds strange, coming from a former convict."

Shauna only had a vague idea of why her uncle had done prison time—something about a fight that ended up with him being charged with manslaughter. She'd never asked, and until now, Davy hadn't talked about it.

His criminal past wasn't so different from her mother's. Deep down, Shauna was glad she'd managed to avoid the same pitfalls. Although, she had fallen for Eric's lies.

"I'm happy for you," Shauna said. "You seem to be at peace."

He grimaced. "As much as I can be, with the burden I carry. God has forgiven me, but it's not so easy to forgive myself."

"I feel the same way about my mom." Shauna's stomach knotted as she remembered her mother's last frantic call and her impatience with yet another crisis.

A real one, not imagined.

Allowing herself to be sucked down into that spiral wasn't healthy, but it wasn't easy to ignore the truth, either. She saw through the back window that Liam was coming back to the squad, so she did her best to stay focused on their next steps.

They needed to understand who was trying to kill her—and soon.

"I'm going to stay here with two deputies to spread out and search the area," Liam informed them. "Deputy Rawson will drive you back to my place."

"Okay." She didn't like it but understood that, as sheriff, Liam had a responsibility to stay at the crime scene. "Although, we can wait here if that's easier, right, Davy?"

"Of course. Shauna is right," Davy agreed. "The more deputies searching for the gunman, the better."

Liam hesitated, then gave a curt nod. "Okay, we'll hold off on driving you back just yet. Keep the doors locked."

Shauna watched as Liam and four deputies spread out around Davy's house with guns drawn and flashlights. She wanted to believe the shooter was long gone, but after Leah's stabbing, she knew there were two men hunting her. And they could both be out there, lying in wait.

A full hour went by before Liam and two of the four deputies returned. She could tell by their dejected expressions that they hadn't found anything helpful.

Liam returned to the squad car and, this time, slid in behind the wheel. "No sign of the shooter. We did find one slug embedded in the side of David's house." He grimaced as he started the car. "Not very helpful unless we get the weapon to match it."

"I'm just glad you weren't hurt." Shauna shivered. "Bold of him to shoot at a cop."

"He may not have realized who I was until I fired back," Liam said. "But, yeah, that only means we can add more charges when we get him in custody."

When, not if. She admired Liam's positive attitude.

"Did you get a good look at him?" Davy asked.

"Enough to believe the shooter was Karl Maxwell," Liam said. "We've issued a BOLO and arrest warrant for him."

Shauna knew that meant every deputy would be on the lookout for Maxwell and that they'd arrest him on sight. She silently prayed that Maxwell would be found very soon.

The ride to Liam's home took another fifteen minutes. She was a bit surprised to realize Liam's modest home was located in an area that was just as isolated as her uncle's.

"David, help me carry the boxes inside," Liam instructed.

She followed Liam and Davy into the house, her curious gaze sweeping the interior. It was more modern than Davy's, and she noticed there were some female touches in the curtains and throw pillows that she felt certain Liam's wife had been responsible for.

Liam and Davy put the boxes in the living room. "I'll throw in a couple of frozen pizzas for dinner."

"I can do that," she offered.

"No need. It will only take a moment." Liam's gaze clashed with hers. "Make yourself comfortable. You and David can fight over the spare bedroom. The other can take the sofa."

"I'll take the sofa," Davy offered without hesitation.

Shauna sighed, knowing arguing would be moot. Her uncle could be stubborn when he wanted to be. And the sofa was probably a step up from his cot in the workshop. She wandered over to the two boxes, opening the one closest to her.

The photographs she'd been hoping to find were right on top. Old pictures of her mother and Davy when she was just a baby. Seeing how young her mother was hit hard. Based on the date scrawled on the back, her mother hadn't even been eighteen yet.

Pregnant at sixteen, giving birth at seventeen. She bit her lip and set the picture aside. The next photograph she found was one of her own school pictures from the fifth grade. Shauna shook her head at the defiant gaze that stared back at her. Even then, she'd carried a chip on her shoulder. Probably because of the clearly hand-me-down clothes she was wearing. Her mother had shopped at secondhand used clothing stores.

As if that had really mattered. Shaking her head at her own stubborn foolishness, she continued poking through the items in the box.

Most of the contents were her school projects. Humbling to realize her mother had bothered to save them. Her awful self-portrait, since she couldn't draw a straight line to save her life, and a short story that had won an award, coming in first place for the entire school. She was so lost in the memories, she didn't notice Liam coming to sit beside her.

"Hey, don't cry." He wrapped his arm around her shoulders.

"I'm not." She swiped at her face to remove the tears that had leaked out without her noticing. "It's just—memories, you know? Some good, some bad, so many I wish I could do over…"

"I know how you feel," Liam murmured.

Of all the men she'd ever known, she felt certain he was right. He'd already mentioned feeling guilty over the loss of his wife and son.

An overwhelming regret they had in common.

She looked up into Liam's compassionate gaze. "Isn't this where you tell me it will get easier in time?"

"It doesn't, not really. But focusing on God's plan for us helps." His gaze dropped to her mouth. Her pulse kicked up with anticipation. When he lowered his head, she lifted her chin to meet him halfway, welcoming his kiss.

A rush of emotions washed over her—elation, joy, gratitude and maybe a twinge of concern.

What was she doing, encouraging Liam's embrace? This wasn't the time to get tangled in a relationship.

"Ah, Liam? Sorry to interrupt, but the oven timer just went off. I think the pizzas are ready."

Davy's voice was like a bucket of cold water dousing them. She jerked back, her cheeks flaming as Liam shot to his feet.

Shauna stayed where she was for a long moment, wishing for something she couldn't have.

It was a bad idea to kiss Shauna while her uncle was in the house. Liam pulled the pizzas out of the oven so quickly he burned his thumb.

Wow, he really needed to get a grip. Maxwell had fired two shots at him just over an hour ago, and the last thing he needed was to let Shauna mess with his head.

With his heart.

His wife had been upset about his long hours, about how isolated they were from the rest of the townsfolk. Yet when Jerica had gotten upset with him, she'd gone back to Madison to visit her parents.

Or so she'd told him, until she'd basically confirmed she was leaving him for another man. He hadn't known until he'd done some investigating that she'd fallen for Sean O'Connor, the Dane County deputy's brother. Which explained why Jason O'Connor had been angry the night of Jerica's car crash and had made it clear he blamed Liam for Jerica's death. He'd been upset on behalf of his brother. Hard to argue, since if he hadn't made a mess of his marriage, his wife and son would still be alive.

He'd probably be divorced, but they'd still be alive.

Liam still had the note she'd left him. Knowing his marriage had crumbled before his eyes was bad enough, but losing Mikey…

The hole in his heart left by the loss of his son would never go away.

And that meant Shauna McKay was off-limits. He couldn't repeat the mistakes of the past. He wasn't going to risk his heart like that again.

He cut the pizzas and placed them in the center of his kitchen table. David and Shauna took seats across from him.

As he sat, David clasped his hands and bowed his head. "Dear Lord, we ask You to bless this food, and to continue watching over us as we seek to bring those who freely break Thy commandments to justice. Amen."

"Amen," Shauna murmured.

"Amen," Liam said. "Thank you, David."

Shauna's uncle inclined his head, then reached for a slice of pizza. "I can't remember the last time I ate pizza," he said with a wry smile. "It's not something the Amish prepare."

"I guess not," Liam agreed. "But it was all I had to offer."

"And it will not go to waste." David took a big bite, clearly enjoying the fare.

"I started going through the first box of Mom's things," Shauna said. "But so far it's mostly stuff she kept from when I was in school."

Liam glanced over to the boxes. He'd hoped they'd find a clue as to who might have hired Karl Maxwell and his dark-haired, burly sidekick, but it didn't sound promising. "All we can do is try."

"I know." Shauna grimaced. "I was really hoping your deputies would have grabbed the blond guy by now."

"Have no fear. God will provide the strength and courage we need," David said.

An old Bible verse—Psalm 23:4—popped into

Liam's mind, something he'd often heard his mother recite. *Yea, though I walk through the valley of the shadow of death, I will fear no evil: for thou art with me; thy rod and thy staff they comfort me.*

"I know you're right," Liam said. "Even if the boxes don't reveal anything helpful, we have to trust that my team of deputies will find Maxwell. Once he's in custody, we can pressure him to tell us who hired him."

Shauna nodded, although her smile didn't quite reach her eyes. They ate in silence for several minutes, Liam eating more than usual, as he'd skipped lunch.

When Shauna finished, she carried her plate to the counter. As she began to fill the sink, he jumped up to stop her. "I'll get those later. Go ahead and keep looking through the boxes."

"Washing dishes is the least I can do," she protested.

"Not tonight. Please, Shauna, sit and relax. It's been a long day for you."

"For you, too," she murmured but obliged him by shutting off the water and heading back into the living room.

He wondered if she was avoiding looking through the boxes because it was difficult for her emotionally. He couldn't blame her. He'd felt the same way when he'd finally cleaned out Mikey's room.

Donating everything to charity.

Turning what was once the nursery into a guest room was the most difficult thing he'd ever done. At least Shauna could use the room to get some badly needed sleep.

David finished eating and, like Shauna, carried his plate and glass to the sink before heading over to join his niece in the living room. Liam was glad the two of them had this time to share their memories, hopefully focusing on the good ones rather than the bad.

Leaving the table, he stored the leftover pizza in the fridge and stacked the dirty dishes before deciding to head outside to look around.

Not that he believed they'd been followed from David's place, but to give Shauna and David some privacy. He tucked his hands into his jacket pockets as he made his way around the house to the backyard. The October wind was brisk, the leaves rustling beneath his feet as he walked.

He used to love autumn, before it became the season when he'd lost his family.

His mind replayed the events outside David's house. Maxwell running away, then turning to shoot at him.

Liam had returned fire while he was on the ground, but the guy managed to change directions at the right time to avoid getting hit. Frustrated, Liam had jumped to his feet to give chase, but by then Maxwell had disappeared into the woods.

He felt certain they'd find a sign of Maxwell hiding, but he and his deputies had only found a set of footprints that they couldn't even say for sure belonged to their perp and the slug embedded in David's house.

Nothing else.

Tomorrow morning, he planned to scour the scene again in the daylight. He knew Maxwell hadn't had time to grab his shell casings, so those were still out there somewhere.

When he felt as if he'd given Shauna and David

enough time, he went back inside. The disappointed expressions on their faces confirmed what he'd feared.

"You didn't find anything?" He eyed them both.

"No." Shauna abruptly stood. "I'm going to try to get some sleep. Good night, Liam. Davy."

She left without saying anything more, but he could tell by the red puffiness of her eyes that she was still upset. Over the contents of the boxes? Or coming up empty-handed?

Likely both.

"This has been a difficult day for her," David said solemnly. "I know the news about how my sister working as a stripper before she had Shauna was a terrible shock."

"Maybe it's not the key to what's going on here," Liam mused wearily. "I mean, twenty-three years is a really long time."

"I still think it is," David insisted. "I know Linda was trying to find Shauna's biological father. And, really, if she was being followed, the way Shauna was, she must have found the man responsible, don't you think?"

"Maybe."

"I wish I'd asked Linda more questions at the time," David said with a sigh. "Obviously she must have known the potential candidates."

"Yeah, well, unfortunately, we may never know." The thought was depressing.

"I pray we learn the truth soon."

Liam's phone rang. Seeing Garrett's name on the screen, he quickly answered it. "Please tell me you found Maxwell."

There was a momentary pause. Then Garrett said, "Yeah, we found him."

"Great. I'll meet you at the station. We'll question him tonight." Liam was already headed into the kitchen when Garrett's voice cut him off.

"No need for that, boss. We found him, but he's dead."

Liam froze in the act of reaching for his jacket. "Dead? How? When?"

"Relatively recent is my guess. Rigor hasn't set in yet. Believe it or not, we found him in the woods at the same location where we found the blood from our John Doe the other day." Garrett paused, then added, "Maxwell was shot in the head, too. The gun is here, at the scene, and we'll have it tested for evidence. I'm expecting it's the same gun that fired those shots at you, boss, but no matter how this looks, I don't believe Maxwell shot himself."

"No, I'm sure he didn't." Liam sank into a chair, a wave of hopelessness hitting hard. "He must have been deliberately silenced. Maybe because he failed to take me out of the picture. Or because they were afraid we'd find him and learn the truth."

"My thoughts exactly," Garrett agreed. "Sorry, boss."

"Yeah, me, too." He lowered his phone, fighting despair.

Maxwell's death wasn't just another murder for them to deal with, which was bad enough.

It also meant they had absolutely no leads on who wanted to kill Shauna.

And at this rate, they might never find the person responsible—until it was too late.

ELEVEN

After a long night of tossing and turning, Shauna got up and dressed in her Amish clothing. The stitches on her forehead had begun to itch, probably an indication the wound was healing. She washed up, then headed into the kitchen. No waiting for coffee to boil on the stove this time, since Liam had an actual coffee maker. She found coffee and gladly made a pot.

Davy was still asleep on the sofa, so she hesitated, unwilling to wake him. Her gaze took in the contents of the boxes they'd left in piles, one for her to take home, not that she had a place to call home any longer. The other one Davy would hang on to for a while.

The items Shauna had decided to keep didn't have any value, but she'd been unable to throw them away, either. The pain of losing her mother was too fresh, and she couldn't bear to part with the few things she had left to remember her by.

The photos were what she treasured the most, even though there weren't more than a handful of them. Five was better than none, although she wished those early memories had been happier times.

What she mostly remembered from her childhood was struggling to survive one day to the next. Some days there would be food on the table; others she'd go to bed hungry. Some days her mother would be in a good mood; other days she'd be drunk and angry. She knew her mother had done her best, but getting involved with alcohol, speed and marijuana hadn't helped.

They'd only made things worse.

Shauna was tiptoeing through the living room toward the boxes when Davy woke up. He blinked and sat up on the sofa. "Good morning, Shauna."

"Good morning. Sorry if I woke you."

"You didn't." He waved that off as he finger combed his hair. "I am usually awake at dawn, so this is sleeping in. I should be getting an early start today. Saturdays are very busy."

"I've started the coffee." Shauna retraced her steps to the kitchen. "Looks like it's almost ready."

Liam joined them shortly thereafter. "Good morning. I hope you both slept well."

"As well as can be expected," Shauna said with a shrug. "It wasn't easy to shut my brain off."

"I can understand, and I'm afraid I have bad news," Liam said as he pulled eggs and milk from the fridge.

She tensed. "About the gunfire last night?"

He set the items on the counter, then turned to face her and Davy. "My chief deputy, Garrett, found Karl Maxwell, but unfortunately, he's dead from a gunshot wound to the temple."

She sucked in a harsh breath. "Just like Jeff Clancy."

Liam inclined his head. "Yes, the same MO. I believe Maxwell was murdered, although we'll need confirmation from the medical examiner on that."

Her knees felt weak. "I don't understand why he was murdered. It doesn't make sense, since he's the one who has been following me."

"I believe his failure to execute the plan is the reason he was silenced." Liam took a moment to break eggs into a bowl. "I hope you like scrambled eggs."

She wasn't the least bit hungry but nodded in agreement. "I still don't see why they would kill him."

"Liam, you mentioned an arrest warrant was issued for Karl Maxwell," Davy said. "Is it possible that's the reason he was killed?"

Liam glanced over his shoulder, his expression somber. "I can't discount the possibility, but that means someone within law enforcement may be involved."

Shauna hadn't thought things could possibly get worse, but she'd been wrong. Sinking into the closest kitchen chair, she stared at him. "Another cop might be involved? Why? How?"

"I guess it's possible someone with a police radio scanner could have heard the news, but the way these guys seem to have access to information has bothered me from the very beginning." Liam whipped the eggs, then added milk. "I don't like it."

She didn't much like it, either. "How many people really use police scanners?"

"More than you'd think, especially out here." He poured the egg mixture into a shallow frying pan. "My reason for telling you this is so you stay alert." He met her gaze. "The danger is far from over."

"Yeah, I kinda got that, even before Maxwell turned

up dead." Despair cloaked her, and she once again thought about leaving Green Lake. Disappearing for a while would probably be better for everyone else in the long run. Poor Leah had already been badly hurt because of her. "Any news on Leah?"

"I'm sure we will learn more regarding Leah's well-being today." Davy rested his hand on her arm. "Don't worry. God is watching over her."

When breakfast was ready, Davy once again said grace. She bowed her head and felt his words reverberate through her. Since coming to Green Lake, living with the Amish, she'd begun to feel God's presence.

And to believe that, maybe, Davy and Liam were right about God watching over them.

The food was great, but Liam refused her help in the kitchen. She decided to clean up the mess in the living room and headed back to where they'd left the empty boxes.

She picked up both boxes, frowning when one seemed heavier than the other. After setting the lighter one down, she felt along the bottom of the heavier box. A slim notebook was wedged between the bottom flaps.

Upon pulling it free, she nearly gasped out loud when she saw it was a diary. Stunned, she sat on the edge of the sofa, then opened it.

Her mother's handwriting had changed over the years, but she recognized the loopy capital *L*s and the extra curlicue on the *Y*s. The date on the first page only listed the month and day, not the year.

April 10th. I started a new job and earned more money in one day than I did in an entire week cleaning rooms at the local motel. Can't tell Mom, though. She'd flip a lid. Good thing she's usually passed out by the time I head to work, so she'll never know. And we need the money.

Shauna closed her eyes, feeling slightly sick. The new job must have been at the strip club. Shauna's birthday was at the end of January, which meant her mother must have gotten pregnant shortly after taking this job.

"What is that?" Davy asked, joining her on the sofa.

"Mom's diary." She looked up at him, her fingers trembling as she held the slim journal. "I'm not sure I can read it without falling apart."

"Would you like me to do that?"

Davy's offer was sweet, but this was her problem, not his. Danger had followed her from Chicago to Green Lake, and a clue to her biological father might be within these pages.

"No, I'll do it." Brave words, but her fingers fumbled a bit as she turned the page.

It wasn't easy to read about her mother's excitement about her job at the strip club, gushing over how much money she made. Even worse, her mother described her private "dates" with men. And she used only first names, not last names, or so it seemed.

Warren and Douglas.

She couldn't finish reading the entries, which outlined the various "dates" she had with each man. That there were more than one with each of them told her everything she needed to know.

She shoved the diary into Davy's hands. "I found

two men who could be my biological father, but I doubt their first names will help much, since they're relatively common names and we have no idea how old they are to narrow the search."

"I'm sorry you had to read this, Shauna, but maybe the names will help." Davy's gaze was worried. "Are you going to be okay?"

She rose to her feet and tried to shake off the churning, twisted feeling in her gut. Her discomfort wasn't important—it was necessary to do whatever possible to make sure her mother's murderer was brought to justice.

Her mother deserved that much. And more.

So much more.

Those two men had taken advantage of her mother's naivete twenty-four years ago. Did that mean her mother deserved to pay for her mistakes with her life?

No. And neither did Shauna. A steely resolve pushed away the nausea.

She wasn't leaving until she found the man responsible.

The best thing she could do for her mother now was to make him, whoever he was, pay for his crimes.

Liam overheard Shauna and David's brief conversation about the two possible biological fathers Linda had identified in her diary.

Only first names, though. He shook his head as he dried the last of the dishes. It was only to be expected, since the men likely wouldn't have given their real last names anyway. If they had, Linda McKay would have had a better idea on where to find them long before now.

It was strange that Shauna's mother hadn't tried to find the two men earlier. Then he straightened. Maybe she had, but with two possible candidates, she had no way of proving one over the other.

Not without forcing a paternity test. Something that might have been difficult if she didn't have money for a good lawyer. And no proof to bring a claim in the first place. He could well imagine no one would believe the word of a woman who worked in a strip club.

"We should head to the Amish Shoppe." David placed a consoling arm around Shauna's shoulders. "Best to keep busy during times like this."

"I need to clean up the mess first." Shauna moved away from Davy and resolutely repacked the boxes with everything they'd removed, except for the diary. "I guess we can take these back to your basement, Uncle Davy. Put mine aside, though, so I can pick it up later."

"Why not just leave them here for now?" Liam suggested. "I don't think heading back to David's after the recent gunfire is a good idea."

She nodded, her features full of grim determination. He was impressed with her strength, her courage. Her sheer determination.

And he wished there was more he could do to help give her some peace of mind.

David was clearly anxious to leave, so he drove them back to the Amish Shoppe. It was still early—the stores didn't open for an hour yet—but he escorted them around back to make sure they were able to get inside safely.

"I'll check in on you later, okay?" he said to Shauna.

"That's fine, although I'm also wondering if I'll be able to visit Leah in the hospital later." She turned toward her uncle. "If they would allow that."

"We'll discuss that possibility with Elizabeth," David assured her.

"I can pick Elizabeth up and give her a ride here," Liam offered.

"She usually is accompanied each morning by one of the elders," David said. "But a ride home tonight would be welcome. Tomorrow is Sunday, so she'll have the protection of the church and her community then."

Liam nodded. "Okay. Be safe." He watched as Shauna and David slipped inside David's workroom before Liam returned to his squad car.

The two men's names rattled around in his head as he drove to headquarters. Two names that could belong to anyone, living anywhere.

Garrett wasn't at his desk when Liam arrived. He strode to his office and grimaced at the mound of paperwork needing his attention.

As sheriff, he was responsible for both patrolling and protecting the community as well as running the jail. Thankfully, he had a wonderful assistant who helped keep the jail running smoothly, and the inmates were usually doing time for nonviolent crimes like DUIs and selling drugs.

He managed to get through a portion of the paperwork before Garrett arrived. His chief deputy came straight to his office. "The medical examiner believes Karl Maxwell was murdered—claims he's right-handed but the bullet entry wound was on the left, so it couldn't have been suicide. There are powder burns and residue around the entry site, same as Clancy."

"I know Maxwell was murdered to keep him from talking," Liam said. "What concerns me is how the killer found out we had issued an arrest warrant for him."

"That's been troubling me, too," Garrett admitted. "Either we have a leak in the department, because that information hadn't hit the news yet, or someone has law enforcement connections."

"Yeah." Liam regarded him steadily. "Any thoughts related to our deputies?"

"Honestly? No," Garrett said. "I get that anything is possible, but they're good guys. I can't imagine they'd leak information about an arrest warrant, especially since we're working a homicide case. Well, two of them now," Garrett corrected.

Liam had the same feeling about his department, but he couldn't afford to ignore the possibility that someone had given out the information in exchange for cash. "From now on, the information on the homicide investigations will be kept between the two of us only. None of the others will be given any further information, understand?"

"Got it. And I agree with your approach, Liam, but keep in mind the original murder was in Chicago, not here." Garrett regarded him steadily. "We know lots of Illinois residents vacation here, especially during the summer months, and several have also purchased summer homes. Not a stretch to think that one of them has a hand in this."

"That's a good point," Liam conceded. "Let's get a

list of all properties owned by Illinois residents. Maybe that's a place to start."

"Will do." Garrett stood. "Anything else?"

Liam grimaced. "Keep your eyes out for a stocky, tall, dark-haired stranger. That's the only perp we're aware of who's still alive."

"You could ask Shauna and Jacy to do another sketch," Garrett suggested.

It wasn't a bad idea, although he didn't have high hopes for the same level of detail she'd been able to provide before. "Go ahead and call Jacy to set it up. I'll ask Shauna to do her best, although I'm not sure she got a good look at him. She did mention his dark hair and beard, but for all we know, he could have shaved by now. The reason she did so well with the first sketch is because she'd seen Maxwell several times on campus, where he'd been following her. Unfortunately, she only had a brief interaction with this assailant."

"Any information is better than none." Garrett left to make the calls.

As the morning wore on, the only additional news he found out was that the caliber of gun retrieved from the scene of Maxwell's death matched the slug they'd taken from David's house. Not a surprise, as that was what he'd expected, but it was good to have it confirmed.

"When will I have the ballistics report?"

"Not until the state crime lab gets around to doing it," his crime scene tech responded.

"Put a rush on it," Liam ordered. "Did you find anything else in the abandoned car belonging to Clancy?"

"Just his fingerprints. No indication anyone else was in the vehicle."

That figured. "Okay, keep me posted if you hear anything further." He sighed, disconnecting from the call.

Garrett poked his head through the doorway to his office. "Jacy can be here in an hour."

"Okay, I'll pick up Shauna." No point in sitting around here. He desperately wanted to find the man who'd stabbed Leah, so he decided to head down to the Amish Shoppe right away.

Not just to see Shauna again, he told himself sternly. But to get a lead on this case.

Yeah, who do you think you're kidding? his inner voice asked sardonically. *Like you wouldn't want to see Shauna regardless of the sketch artist coming to the station.*

He did his best to ignore it.

After sliding behind the wheel of the squad car, he headed out of town. He chose a circular route around the lake, keeping an eye out for anything unusual.

He slowed down near the section of highway where both Clancy's and Maxwell's bodies were found. Crime scene tape still cordoned off the area, but he wasn't staffed to the point he could stick a deputy here to keep an eye on the place.

Besides, they'd already removed any evidence worth protecting.

There were no vehicles behind him as he continued making his way toward the Amish Shoppe. When he approached the parking lot, he wasn't surprised to see it was jam-packed with cars.

Tourists knew that today was the day to shop, as the Amish did not work on Sunday. Come Monday, the crowds would be smaller and more manageable.

The only empty spots were near the highway, so he pulled in and got out to walk. He was about halfway to the red barn when he glimpsed movement from the corner of his eye.

A black pickup truck roared to life, the driver barreling out of the parking space with careless disregard for pedestrians. When Liam noticed the driver had dark hair and bulky shoulders, he ran after the truck.

"Stop! Police!" he shouted as he tried to gain on the vehicle.

The driver's response was to hit the gas, the truck lurching forward. He knew he wouldn't be able to catch it on foot, but he continued following, trying to make out the license plate while using his radio to alert his deputies.

"Black Ford pickup truck, leaving the Amish Shoppe heading west. Suspect behind the wheel could be our perp. License plate is from Illinois but is covered with mud. First digit could be a four, but the rest is not visible. Repeat, black Ford pickup with mud-spattered Illinois license plates heading west on Highway double Y."

Even as the last words left his mouth, the black pickup truck vanished behind a curve. He kept running, though, reaching his car in record time.

He quickly started the engine and gave chase, red lights and sirens blaring as he followed the truck.

Liam expected to come up on the truck fairly quickly, but as his car ate up the miles, he had a sinking feeling in his chest that he'd somehow missed it.

But how? There weren't that many side streets going off the main highways in this area.

He ground his teeth together when he met up with his deputy coming in from the other direction. They parked side by side, and Liam rolled down his window so they could talk.

"Where did it go?" Deputy Edgerton asked.

Liam scowled. "I have no idea. I guess he could have gone through the fields, but I didn't see any sign of that."

"Let's swing past to double-check."

Liam made a U-turn and drove slowly down the highway, searching both sides of the road to see if he could find where the black truck may have gone.

When he saw some tire treads imprinted on the grass, he pulled over and followed them through the harvested cornfield.

There was another highway on the other side of the acreage, but when he looked both ways, the road was empty of traffic.

He sighed.

If this was the path the black Ford had taken, the vehicle was long gone.

TWELVE

Shauna smiled at the customer who'd just purchased one of Davy's kitchen tables. It was a huge and badly needed boon for his business, but her mind was a million miles away.

The blond guy, Maxwell, was dead. Murdered. And her mother had been on several private dates with two men who could possibly have gotten Linda pregnant.

And one of them was likely her biological father.

"Shauna, your being here has been a true blessing." Davy emerged from his workroom with his dark hair covered in sawdust, a broad grin creasing his face. "Maybe it's your beautiful smile that has drawn these customers in when I've needed them the most."

"Aw, Davy." She hugged him tight. "That's a sweet thing to say, but your incredible workmanship speaks for itself."

"Your influence, I'm sure." He held her for a long moment before letting go. He searched her gaze. "No sign of the dark-haired man who stabbed Leah?"

"Not yet, and trust me, I've been watching. Unfortunately, I didn't get a good look at him, so I've been searching for anyone who is big and burly."

Davy's grin faded. "Liam and his deputies will find him."

"I hope you're right. Leah didn't deserve this." She couldn't shake her concern over how Leah had been hurt when Shauna was the intended target.

"*Denke*, Shauna, for sending that last couple to my store." Elizabeth crossed over to join them. "*Sehr gut*, they purchased two of my quilts. 'Tis a *gut* day, ain't so?"

"I'm glad to hear it." Shauna didn't see any resentment in Elizabeth's gaze over the role she'd played in Leah's injury. "I still wish there was something I could do to help Leah."

"*Ach*, we are a supportive community, certain sure, and several women have stepped in to help manage the Sunshine Café," Elizabeth assured her. "I will let them know we are available to help as needed, *ja*?"

"I'd like that, thanks." She hesitated. "Is Leah accepting visitors at the hospital?"

"Don't worry. Her family is with her." Elizabeth patted her hand. "'Tis not your fault, Shauna."

Shauna didn't believe her. "I'm sure Leah doesn't see it that way."

"Leah's family harbors no ill will toward you, Shauna. We turn to God in times of trouble rather than placing blame."

"Thank you, Elizabeth." She was humbled by the woman's faith, in God and in the Amish community. "I would like to visit Leah when she's feeling up to it."

Elizabeth nodded. "*Sehr gut*. We will make bread for her family."

Shauna had no clue how to bake anything, but she

understood they couldn't arrive empty-handed. "I'm happy to learn how to bake bread."

"Shauna?" Liam's voice drew her gaze, and her heart gave a betraying thump when she saw him. Her awareness of this man was off the charts, and she needed to get past it. At least she knew he wasn't lying to her about being a widower, yet she couldn't allow these feelings for him to flourish. If they ever figured out who was trying to kill her, she couldn't imagine staying in a small town like Green Lake. She had her degree to finish, after all.

Then again, she wasn't looking forward to finding a new place to live and getting a new job. But to be honest, the prospects for both were likely much better in the Chicago area than here.

"Hi, Liam." She frowned when she noticed the strain on his features. "What's wrong?"

"Did you notice anything suspicious?"

"No. Why?" She glanced at Davy and Elizabeth, who both shook their heads. "It's been a good day as far as people buying."

"I'd like you to come down to work with Jacy Urban again," Liam said without directly answering her question. "We need a sketch of the man who stabbed Leah."

"Liam, I didn't get a clear look at his face. The stabbing is nothing more than a blur. I noticed his stature more than anything." She hated disappointing him but felt bad wasting his time, too. "I'm sorry. You know I'd do anything to help."

"I'm asking you to try, Shauna. If the sketch doesn't turn out helpful, that's fine, but it's better than nothing." He hesitated, then added, "I may have gotten a glimpse of him driving away from here in a black Ford pickup truck."

"He was here at the Amish Shoppe?" She paled. "I didn't see him, or if I did, I didn't recognize him."

"He might not have come all the way inside," Liam pointed out. "The parking lot is jam-packed with cars. The number of people here might have scared him off. He must have seen me, because the truck suddenly started and he bolted out of the parking spot. By the time I jumped into the squad to follow, he was gone."

She battled another wave of despair. It seemed that every time they got close, the bad guys managed to escape. She forced herself to nod in agreement. "I'll try to help with the sketch. Just—don't expect too much."

"I only ask that you do your best," Liam said with a weary smile. He held out his hand. "Ready?"

"Yes." She placed her hand in his, the warmth of his fingers giving her a spurt of determination. If there was any chance she could help find the man who stabbed Leah, she'd give it her best.

Shauna followed Liam down the center aisle as he wove through the crowds. There were so many people, no one paid much attention to them. Her Amish dress provided an unusual anonymity. Not that she ever wore clothing intended to garner male attention, but the way people looked right past her was a bit disconcerting.

The dark-haired man hadn't, though, she reminded herself. He'd boldly stepped between them, lashing out with his knife, cutting Leah when he'd really meant to hurt or kill Shauna.

When they were settled in the squad car, she asked, "Did you get a license plate number from the Ford?"

"The plate was covered with mud, but I was able to see enough to recognize it was an Illinois plate. And the first digit is possibly the number four, or maybe the letter *A*." He grimaced. "I'm not happy he managed to get away."

"You'll find him." She silently prayed her sketch would help with that.

"We will. He'll make a mistake at some point." He glanced at her. "Did you talk to Elizabeth about staying with her tonight?"

"Yes. She assured me I'm welcome to stay. She also explained that the community would notice a car driving around, as that's a rare occurrence." She reluctantly smiled. "Except for you, Liam. Elizabeth said her mother-in-law knew all about you dropping us off, as several women mentioned it."

"I'm sure they did," he said wryly. "The Amish community knows my parents left years ago, and I think they tolerate me because of the family connection."

"I thought the Amish shunned those who left."

"Some of the stricter Amish communities might, but thankfully Bishop Bachman preaches a more forgiving countenance."

"I'm glad." One thing this nightmare had taught her was to cherish her family. A lesson she wished she'd learned earlier.

When they arrived at the station, Shauna was escorted to the same room she and Jacy had used before. The work was harder this time, though, as she struggled to come up with distinguishing features.

"You're doing great, Shauna," Jacy encouraged.

"I'm not, but only because I didn't see him clearly."

She sighed. "Let's try the eyes slightly closer together and the eyebrows thicker."

By the time they'd finished, Shauna eyed the resulting sketch with a sinking heart. It wasn't nearly as good as the first one. "I can't think of anything else to change," she said apologetically.

Liam came over to see the final product. "Thanks, Shauna. This will help."

She didn't see how that was possible, but there wasn't anything she could do to fix it. "I hope so."

"I'll drive you back to the Amish Shoppe," he said, handing the sketch over to Garrett.

"We'll get this sketch out with the BOLO and vehicle description," Garrett said. "The combination should help narrow the list of suspects."

His statement helped buoy her mood. Maybe her sketch would help them find the Ford pickup truck. It couldn't hurt.

"Garrett, once you get that sketch out, see if you can narrow down any black Ford pickup trucks starting with the number four or letter *A* from Illinois."

"I've run that DMV list, boss, but it's long." Garrett grimaced. "Five pages with twenty-five license plates and names each."

"Okay. See if you can narrow that down by a man with the first name of Warren or Douglas." Liam glanced at her. "I know it's not likely the guy is coming after you himself, but he may still own the vehicle."

"Got it." Garrett left with the sketch.

Shauna stared at his retreating figure. "You trust him, right?"

"I do," Liam said. "He's been here longer than I

have, since he started as a rookie. Honestly, he'd make a good sheriff someday if I decide to call it quits."

That comment shocked her. "Why would you do that?"

He shrugged and steered her back outside. "I'm not saying I'd leave, but this is an elected position. The town trusts those who grew up here."

"Like you," she said.

He grimaced. "I lived in Madison for a while— that's where I met my wife—but then I came back to Green Lake, as I thought it would be a nice place to raise a family." His expression hardened. "Turned out I was wrong."

"You weren't wrong, Liam." She gazed out the window as they left the center of town to head into the more rural area. "It's just that some people aren't built for living out in the country without a lot of people around. It's possible your wife was one of them."

He didn't respond as he kept one eye on the rearview mirror. He was so intent, she turned in her seat to look through the back window.

There weren't any cars on the road behind them for as far as she could see.

As she turned back to face the front, the sun emerged from behind a dark cloud. The sudden brightness made her eyes hurt, and she lifted her hand to shield them.

At the same moment, a shot rang out, followed by a metallic ping as a bullet hit their car.

"Get down!" Liam shouted as he wrestled to keep the car on the road.

She ducked down in the seat, her heart thudding against her ribs as she prayed for God to keep them safe.

* * *

Liam had caught the flash of light coming from the trees seconds before hearing the sound of gunfire. He punched the accelerator with his foot, grimly ignoring the check-engine light that flashed on the dash.

The bullet had struck the front of the car. Not good, especially since the flash he'd seen was the sun reflecting off a rifle scope.

Grabbing the radio, he quickly called for backup. "This is unit one. Shots fired off Highway YY. My squad is hit. Repeat, officer needs assistance."

"Ten-four, Sheriff."

Despite his foot pressing the accelerator to the floor, their speed slowed. He gritted his teeth, mentally urging the car to keep going. They were too vulnerable out here.

"Why are we slowing down?" Shauna asked.

"Engine is hit. We may have a leak in the radiator." As soon as the words left his mouth, smoke began to billow from beneath the hood.

He wrenched the squad car over to the side of the road. "Stay down," he warned as he pushed out of the car.

"Wait! Where are you going?" Shauna's tone was panicked.

"We're going to use the squad for cover." He pushed against his door, mentally prepared for another barrage of gunfire.

He wasn't disappointed.

He didn't get out but shut the door and bent over the center console, determined to protect Shauna as more bullets pinged against the metal. The moment the gunfire stopped, though, he lunged from the vehicle and darted around to the opposite side.

The shooter was perched in the woods across the cornfield on the driver's side. He wrenched open Shauna's door. "Come on. I want you to hide behind the car engine. That's the safest place for you."

She awkwardly got out of the car and hunkered down behind the front of the car. Seconds later, the windshield shattered into millions of pieces.

"Where is he?" Shauna asked. "I don't see him!"

"That's because he's perched in a tree, shooting at us with a long-range rifle." He kept his head down while covering Shauna with his body. "Just stay down. Our backup will be here any minute."

She fell silent, but he was so close he could feel her body trembling with fear. He was angry with himself for not anticipating that this guy would formulate a new plan. They were on the main highway leading from Green Lake to the Amish Shoppe. After their earlier near miss, the dark-haired guy had obviously decided to ambush them from afar.

Shooting at a cop, a sheriff, reeked of desperation. And that fact alone was concerning.

Whoever had hired these guys wasn't messing around. They intended to kill Shauna.

No matter how many of them died trying.

Shauna's whispered prayers touched his heart, and he wanted to reassure her that he wouldn't let anything happen to her. He'd sacrifice himself if necessary.

Before he could say anything, though, the wail of sirens indicated his backup had arrived. Reassured, he peeked over the roof of the car, trying to locate the shooter's location.

Thankfully, he didn't hear further gunfire, but that only made him think the guy was on the move.

"Stay here," he told Shauna. "I'm going after him."

"No, wait…" she protested, but it was too late. He was already up and making his way around the front of the squad car, weapon in hand.

He wasn't going to allow this guy to get away. Not this time.

It was risky to go after him. The recently harvested cornfield didn't offer any cover. Liam ran as fast as possible, moving in a zigzag manner, braced for the sound of gunfire and the painful impact of a bullet.

But all he could hear was the wail of approaching sirens.

Since he reached the woods without suffering another attack, he felt certain the shooter had already left the scene. Still, he moved into the brush, searching for signs the perp might have left behind.

He stopped short when he saw a heel print in the earth among the bed of fallen leaves. It was deep, as if the guy had pushed off with his foot. Surveying the area, he felt certain the guy had been running away, so he turned to head back toward a cluster of trees.

Only one of them had branches low enough for a tall guy to grab and use to swing himself up. Liam took a moment to examine the ground and found two more boot prints. As if the guy had dropped from the branch, landing hard.

This had to be the location the shooter had used.

Rather than climbing the tree, he turned to follow the path he believed the perp had taken.

It was a nearly impossible task—the leaves, pine needles and fallen tree branches made it difficult to find boot prints. Just when he was about to give up, he crouched down, eyeing an indentation in the dirt.

Deep, like the others, reinforcing his belief that the guy had been running.

But headed where? He swept his gaze over the dense woods. No place to leave a vehicle. Not even a pickup truck.

He pushed forward, hoping to find something useful. After emerging from a thick line of trees, he stopped short.

A black leather glove was on the ground. Left by the shooter? Or a random hiker?

It looked too new and undamaged by the elements to have been there for long. He drew an evidence bag from his pocket and collected the glove, praying there might be usable DNA inside.

He was so intent on securing the evidence, he didn't hear the rustle of leaves. But the blast of gunfire, followed seconds later by a bullet smashing into the ground inches from his left foot, got his attention. Survival instincts had him ducking and rolling toward the closest tree in the nick of time.

"Police! Come out with your hands up!"

The only response was another gunshot. Liam instinctively returned fire in the general direction the shot had come from, more so to keep the perp from shooting again. He didn't want to kill this guy—he wanted him alive and talking.

Thankfully, he still had his radio. "Shots fired. Perp is hiding in the woods. I need all deputies on deck to find him."

"Roger that," Garrett's voice responded.

Liam didn't like being pinned down, but the shooter had the advantage of having a scope on his rifle.

He remained where he was, watching for any hint of movement.

He tried calling out again. "Police! Come out with your hands on top of your head!"

Still no response. He hadn't expected one—this guy had already shot at his squad car, then directly at him, not caring he was law enforcement.

No reason to believe he'd surrender now.

In the distance, he could hear his deputies crossing the field and entering the woods, their footsteps loud amid the crunchy leaves covering the ground. Yet Liam remained where he was, patiently watching for movement.

The seconds ticked by slowly, but he remained calm, his attention laser focused on the cluster of trees located about thirty yards from him.

There! Just the slightest bit of movement. He fired his weapon well above the spot where he estimated the guy's head to be, hoping to scare him into giving up. Liam waited for what seemed like forever.

Then the leaves rustled and the dark-haired guy staggered from the cover of the trees. Liam sucked in a breath when he realized he was clutching his abdomen, the rifle dangling from one hand.

"Drop your weapon!" Liam shouted, convinced this was nothing more than a clever ruse to draw him out.

He didn't think he could have actually hit him. For sure not with the second shot that he'd purposefully aimed well over his head, but maybe the first one? He gritted his teeth. "Now!"

The guy let go of the gun, which fell silently to the earth. Then his knees buckled and he slid to the ground, too.

Liam watched for several long moments as the perp lay unmoving. Then he risked coming out from his hiding spot and darting over to him.

After kicking the rifle well out of reach, he knelt and grabbed the guy's wrist, wrenching it behind his back. He quickly reached for the other wrist, cuffing them together, before he rolled him over.

A sinking sensation hit hard. Dark blood stained the front of his camouflage shirt where the bullet had struck his abdomen. He quickly felt for a pulse. It was there, but weak.

"Perp has been hit with gunfire to his belly. I need a medical chopper here now!" he shouted through his radio. "And help getting him out of the woods. Hurry!"

"Ten-four," came the response.

Liam shucked his jacket, balled it up and pressed it against the dark-haired guy's abdominal wound, using all his weight to add pressure. He would do whatever was necessary to slow or stop the bleeding.

The dark-haired guy was still alive. And Liam needed him to stay that way.

THIRTEEN

Waiting was torture. Shauna hated every minute of being held back, protected by Deputy Sanders while Liam disappeared into the woods, searching for the gunman. Sanders kept her behind the damaged squad car, protecting her back while the other deputies fanned out to follow Liam.

Then she'd heard the sharp retort of gunfire, and her heart had lodged in her throat, making it impossible to breathe. To cry. To scream.

All she could do was pray.

Please, Lord, please keep Liam safe!

She hadn't earned the right to ask God for help, but that didn't stop her from trying. She had never learned about the Bible and God's teaching, not until she'd heard Elizabeth reading from the Bible. And Liam and Davy had both told her about how they were in God's hands and that He had a plan for them. They also said God was full of grace and mercy.

She prayed God would have mercy on Liam now.

Deputy Sanders's radio crackled, and when she heard Liam's voice explaining the gunman was injured, she sagged against the car and closed her eyes in relief.

"Ambulance is already on the way," Sanders said. "I'll get the trauma alert out, too."

Shauna rose to her feet, moving away from the squad car. Sanders frowned at her while he spoke on his radio to the dispatcher.

"The gunman can't hurt me anymore," she said when Sanders finished. "I'm safe enough."

"The sheriff expects us to protect you," Sanders argued. "If something happens, it's my job on the line."

"I know. I'm not going anywhere, but I need to stretch." She'd been crouched behind the car for what seemed like hours, although she knew it wasn't. She swung her arms and stamped her feet to get the circulation moving in her limbs.

More minutes passed until an ambulance careened toward them, red lights flashing. When the driver pulled off behind the squad car, Sanders hurried over to provide an update.

"One victim of a gunshot wound in the field. Trauma call went out for a chopper."

"We'll help stabilize him until the chopper arrives," the EMT said.

In the distance, Shauna could see several deputies and Liam carrying a man out of the woods. One of them had a rifle tucked under his arm, and she figured it must have belonged to the gunman. "There they are." She gestured toward them.

"Let's go." The two EMTs pulled their gurney out of the ambulance, then hurried over to meet up with the deputies. Watching them working together to save this man's life was humbling.

Even from here, she could see Liam's grim expression. She'd heard the gunfire and knew he must have fired at least once, hitting the suspect. When they had the guy on the gurney, she brushed past Sanders to meet up with them.

"Hey, where are you going?" Sanders asked, hurrying to catch up. He grabbed her arm to hold her back. Maybe he was worried she'd do something erratic, but that wasn't the case.

"Let go. I need to get a good look at the gunman's face." She shook off Sanders's hand and moved forward. The guy on the gurney was pale, but he had dark hair and a bulky build. She stared at his slack facial features, which sort of resembled her sketch. "Yes, that's him," she said with certainty. Her gaze collided with Liam's. "This is the man who stabbed Leah."

"Thanks for the positive ID." Liam's features were drawn, and she knew he must be feeling guilty for shooting him. She didn't know exactly what had happened in the woods, but she knew with complete certainty that Liam wouldn't have fired his gun at this man unless it was necessary.

Thankfully, he was still alive. But for how long? She didn't know anything about survival rates for gunshot wounds to the abdomen.

The EMTs did their thing, hooking the dark-haired man to a heart monitor, starting an IV and adding thick gauze to his wound. In the distance, she heard the *whomp, whomp, whomp* of the chopper.

"They're not going to let us ride along." Garrett gestured toward the chopper that was making its descent. "There's a weight limit."

"I know. We'll meet up with them at the hospital. His condition is serious enough that I'm sure they'll end up taking him straight to surgery, so it's not like we'll be able to question him, even if he was conscious, which he isn't." Liam shook his head wearily. "I pray he survives."

"He will," Garrett assured him.

Liam turned to glance at her. "Shauna? You're okay?"

"I'm fine." She searched his gaze. "I know you're probably going straight to the hospital, and I'd like to go with you."

He was shaking his head before she'd finished speaking. "I don't think that's a good idea. I'll have Deputy Sanders take you back to the Amish Shoppe." Liam turned to look at the deputy holding the rifle. "Get that to the crime scene techs. I want those prints in the system as soon as possible. We need this guy's name."

"Will do, boss." The deputy holding the rifle by the tip of the barrel hurried over to one of the squad cars to set the gun in the trunk.

"Please, Liam." She caught his gaze. "The danger has been averted for now. You've caught the gunman, right? And while there's still a lot we don't know, a busy hospital would provide better security than what they have at the Amish Shoppe." She paused, then added, "Besides, I'd really like to stop in to see Leah. To apologize and to offer any support I can."

"Her family is with her," Liam said with a frown. "The Amish take care of their own."

"I know." She couldn't deny feeling a hint of dread at facing them. "I owe them an apology, too."

The chopper lifted off, banking to the left to head to the closest trauma center. For several long moments, no one spoke.

"Fine," Liam finally said. "We'll go to the hospital together." Liam gestured to Garrett. "Will you take care of getting the squad towed? And I'd like to use your SUV, if that's okay."

"That's fine. I'll catch a ride with Sanders." Garrett tossed Liam the keys. "I'll need some time before I meet up with you at the hospital."

"Okay. Call me if you learn anything." Liam took her arm, guiding her toward the SUV. "I shouldn't be bringing you along," he said, half under his breath.

"Why not?" She glanced at him before sliding into the passenger seat. "I don't see how visiting the hospital goes against the rules."

"I'm on official police business," he pointed out. "Not that I think our suspect will be talking anytime soon." He shut the door and jogged around to the other side.

She wasn't sure what to say to that, so she remained silent as Liam drove to the hospital. She'd expected lights and sirens, but he didn't use them. Thankfully, the overall traffic seemed light.

"I'm sorry you had to shoot him," she said, breaking the silence.

"I didn't intend to hit him." Liam's tone was grim, and he rubbed his hand over his face. "He shot first. When he fired again a second time, I instinctively returned fire to prevent him from coming after me again. He stayed in the trees for a while, probably waiting for a second chance to hit me, but then he came out, holding his belly…"

She reached out to touch his arm. "He'll be okay."

Liam gave a tense nod but didn't say anything more. She understood his moral dilemma. Yes, he'd been under fire, more than once, considering the squad car had been hit several times even before the gunman fired at him in the woods. But causing harm to a human being wasn't something anyone wanted to do. Not unless they absolutely had to.

"Pray with me." Liam's abrupt request caught her off guard, but she readily clasped his hand. "Lord God, please spare this man's life. Amen."

"Amen," she added. She kept her hand on his as a silent show of support. "I take it we still don't know his name?"

"No, but once we get his fingerprints in the system, I'm hoping we will."

"If he has an arrest record."

"Yeah. Maxwell did, so I'm thinking this guy probably will, too. It makes sense that whoever hired these guys chose them specifically because of their criminal backgrounds." He glanced at her. "Try not to worry about it. We'll figure out who hired him and why."

"It's hard to imagine my biological father doing something like this." She frowned. "I don't see how my mother could have been a serious threat to him. Or to anyone, really. She was more of a harm to herself."

"Keep in mind, she was only sixteen back then," Liam said gently.

She winced. "Yeah, but he probably didn't know that. I mean, why would he? Davy said she used a fake ID to get hired at the strip club in the first place. They can't be held responsible for not knowing the truth."

"Most likely," Liam agreed.

They arrived at the hospital a few minutes later. The place was bigger than she'd imagined, considering the population of Green Lake wasn't that large. Liam parked the SUV and they walked inside.

Here, unlike the Amish Shoppe, her plain dress, apron and *kapp* drew much attention. She told herself to ignore the curious gazes and felt bad knowing this was what the Amish endured on a regular basis.

Mostly the looks were simply curiosity, but there were some derogatory expressions as well. As if choosing the plain and simple life was something to be looked down upon.

To her shame, she felt certain that might have been her attitude, too. Before she really understood what the Amish were all about.

Davy's words echoed in her mind. *When you give up technology and the distractions that go along with it, you begin to understand what is important. Like having a closer relationship with God and, of course, with your family.*

Yes, the more time she spent with the Amish, the more she understood they were stronger than most people she'd encountered in her life.

Stronger in faith, and in spirit.

They deserved to be admired, not that they were seeking that from the outside world. All they wanted was to be left alone to raise their families as they saw fit. To survive and thrive.

Wasn't that what she'd wanted, too?

"Stay here for a minute," Liam said.

"Okay." She took a seat in the emergency department waiting room while he went to find information on his suspect. It didn't take him long to return.

"He's in surgery," he said. "And he remains in critical condition."

"He'll pull through this, Liam. Trauma doctors are very good at what they do."

"Yeah, I know." His smile appeared forced. "You mentioned visiting Leah. She's up on the third floor."

"Let's head up there, then." She tried not to let her reluctance show. This was why she'd insisted on coming, and it was the right thing to do.

Not easy, but right.

Liam escorted her to the third floor, but when he moved to follow, she put a hand on his arm. "I'll take it from here. Better I face them alone."

"Okay. I need to make a few calls anyway." He glanced around. "Why don't you meet me down in the lobby? Where we came in?"

"I will." She swallowed hard and forced herself to walk toward Leah's room. The door was closed, but she could hear the murmur of voices inside.

She paused outside the door, then lifted her hand to knock. She heard something like *"Komm,"* so she turned the handle and went inside.

The room held at least six people hovering around Leah's hospital bed. She recognized Ezekiel Moore, the elder who'd given her and Elizabeth a ride to the Amish Shoppe, and realized he must be Leah's grandfather. The family looked at her in surprise, except for Leah and Ezekiel, who recognized her.

"My name is Shauna McKay, and I'm here to apologize for Leah being hurt. The man who stabbed her did so by mistake. I was the one he was looking for. I'm the one who should be here, in the hospital." She felt her eyes well up with tears. "I'm truly sorry, Leah. I know I'm to blame, and if there's anything I can do, please let me know."

For a long moment no one said a word. Then Leah spoke. "*Ach*, Shauna, 'tis not your fault, but the hand of the man wielding the knife, *ja*?"

Surprisingly, her family members nodded in agreement. Ezekiel added, "We are grateful for your concern."

Shauna bowed her head, feeling blessed by their forgiveness.

Thank You, Lord!

Liam waited on hold while Garrett put a rush on getting the victim's fingerprints into the system. "Okay, looks like we have a hit," Garrett said. "Pete Norman, age thirty-five, did prison time for aggravated assault with a deadly weapon."

The news wasn't a surprise. "Is he an Illinois resident?"

"Yep, last known address in Chicago." He heard the clacking of computer keys. "He doesn't own a black Ford pickup truck, though. The vehicle on record with the DMV is a Honda Civic."

"Of course not—that would be too easy," Liam muttered. "I need you to search for connections between Maxwell and Norman. These guys must have done time together or something. We need to understand who may have hired them."

"On it," Garrett agreed. "I haven't shared this information with anyone else. Just in case there is a leak somewhere."

"Thanks." Liam thought about that for a moment. "If the person who hired Norman doesn't realize he's been injured, we may have some extra time to investigate."

"Maybe," Garrett agreed. "Although we did use the radio to discuss the gunfire and the perp being wounded."

The brief flash of relief faded. "You're right." He sighed heavily. "I hate thinking that someone within law enforcement might be involved."

"Or someone with connections," Garrett countered. "We have no real proof that a cop is involved. Anyone could get access to a police scanner."

"I know, I know." He tried to think through this logically. "I just hope we get a break from the gunfire long enough for us to figure out who is behind this."

"And who the next hired gun might be," Garrett added. "Because you know this isn't over."

"Very true." Not a happy thought. "Keep me updated on anything you uncover. Especially if there's a man by the name of Warren or Douglas involved."

"I've been going through the list of black Ford trucks. So far I haven't found any owned by a man named Warren or Douglas," Garrett admitted. "I'll keep looking, though."

"Thanks. I know the leads are slim, but that's all we have for now." Liam didn't think he'd ever been involved in a more frustrating case.

"Are you heading back here?" Garrett asked.

"Yes." Liam glanced at his watch. "Shauna is visiting Leah. I'll drop her off at the Amish Shoppe and then come back in. I know it's Saturday, but all overtime will be approved."

"The guys would work without the extra pay," Garrett said. "Anyone shooting at one of us deserves to be held to the full extent of the law."

A faint smile creased his features. "Thanks, Garrett, but assure them that while I appreciate the sentiment, they'll be duly compensated for the extra hours they've worked."

"Okay, see you later."

Liam disconnected from the call and glanced at his watch again. He was feeling impatient, but Shauna deserved to have some time with Leah. He felt just as bad as Shauna about how Leah was injured.

The only good thing to come out of the early-afternoon events was that they'd found the man who'd hurt Leah. When, not *if,* he recovered, Pete Norman would do jail time for another assault with a deadly weapon.

Along with the attempted murder of a cop.

He paced the length of the lobby, thinking about whether he should take Shauna and David back to his place again or go back to the original plan of having her stay with Elizabeth.

Putting his cousin in danger didn't sit well. Especially after Leah's injury.

His phone rang, and he quickly answered. "Harland."

"Sheriff, this is the ER doc you spoke to earlier," the female voice said.

"Yes, Dr. Olson." His stomach clenched. "Do you have news related to our gunshot wound victim? His name is Pete Norman, by the way."

"Yes. I wanted to let you know his condition has been stabilized," she said. "The word came down from the OR that they'll need an ICU bed for him after surgery."

"Thanks, I appreciate that." Liam had requested to know if their victim would be admitted, as he intended to have a deputy sitting at his bedside. Norman might be injured, but he was still in police custody. And it wasn't unheard-of for victims to attempt to escape while being in the hospital. "Do you have a time frame? I'll need to get a deputy up from Green Lake to sit with him."

"The OR staff indicated he'd probably be transferred over in an hour," she said. "I hope that's enough
time for you."

"It is, thanks." He quickly called Garrett back.
"Norman will be finished up in surgery within the
hour. They're planning to admit him to the ICU. I want
a deputy at his bedside 24/7."

"Got it. Turmick offered to take the first shift."

"Works for me, thanks." Liam lowered the phone,
impressed by his team's willingness to chip in, even
on the weekend. He didn't want to believe any of them
could be the source of the information leak.

Yet Maxwell had been killed for a reason. Someone
thought he'd break down and talk after being arrested.

If only he hadn't returned fire, injuring Norman.
They could be interrogating him right now, and planning to go after the person responsible, rather than
waiting for him to get out of surgery.

At least the guy had survived. Liam silently thanked
God for that.

Then he glanced at his watch again. Only twenty
minutes had gone by, but he'd expected Shauna to be
here by now. The Amish elders spoke mostly in Pennsylvania Dutch, although some had learned English
words out of necessity. The younger generation were
more fluent in the English language—a requirement
when selling goods to the tourists in the area.

Liam waited another painstaking five minutes before
striding to the elevator. His nerves were on edge, and with
good reason. He'd only fired his weapon a few times in
the line of duty, and he'd never seriously injured a suspect.

Until today.

On the third floor, he looked up and down the hallway but didn't see Shauna. Had he missed her in the lobby? Maybe she'd used the restroom.

To double-check, he strode down toward Leah's room. The door was open, but he knocked anyway.

"Komm," a weak female voice said.

"Leah?" He smiled at the group of family surrounding her. "I'm sorry to bother you. I'm looking for Shauna."

The Amish exchanged concerned glances. Finally Leah said, "Shauna left a while ago. Mayhap ten minutes?"

The tiny hairs on the back of his neck lifted in alarm. "Thank you." He spun on his heel and headed back down to the lobby.

He walked the length of the lobby but didn't see any sign of Shauna. Turning, he went to the public restrooms, hovering near the doorway until a woman stepped out.

"Excuse me, but I'm looking for my friend Shauna. She's wearing a dark blue Amish dress, white apron and white hat. Is she inside?"

"No. I'm sorry. I was the only one inside."

Liam waited until she left, then opened the door to check for himself.

It was empty. He returned to the lobby, his heart thudding painfully in his chest.

Where was Shauna?

FOURTEEN

Leah's family had prayed for her.

Shauna had been caught off guard when Leah's entire family had bowed their heads, praying out loud for her safety as well as for Leah's quick healing. They'd spoken in the lyrical Pennsylvania Dutch, yet she'd recognized many of the words, either from context or those she'd learned from Elizabeth.

That a group of strangers, people she'd never met before, cared about her enough to pray over her was amazing.

Humbled in the presence of their faith, Shauna hadn't known what to say or do. All she could manage was to offer a heartfelt thanks before quickly leaving the hospital room. Instead of taking the elevator, though, to return to the lobby, she'd chosen to take the stairs. She'd wanted some time alone, without other people nearby, to absorb the experience.

There weren't enough words to describe the various emotions reeling through her. All she could think about was how grateful she was for this opportunity she'd been given, experiencing life within the Amish community.

Her intent had been to apologize to Leah, but instead she'd gotten far more than she'd deserved in return. She hoped to have time later to talk to Elizabeth, to try to understand more about the Amish culture and their beliefs.

Maybe she could even learn some Pennsylvania Dutch.

The stairwell she'd taken led all the way outside. It wasn't her intent, but now that she was here, she saw the sidewalk leading around the building to a side street. She walked in that direction, still thinking about what had transpired upstairs.

A crisp October breeze cooled her flushed cheeks. She lifted her face to the partially cloudy sky, thinking about God. About how much she'd heard about Him in the short time she'd been in Green Lake. She wished her mother was still alive, not just so she could make amends, but to help her mother find God the way Davy had.

The way she was beginning to.

So many regrets, yet there wasn't anything she could do about them now. Except to learn from her mistakes, of which she'd made many. Time to focus on the importance of family—and she made a silent promise to stay in touch with Davy once this nightmare was over.

After a few minutes, she'd pulled herself together enough to put the past to rest. Liam was waiting for her in the lobby, and she knew they had to get back to the Amish Shoppe to pick up Davy and Elizabeth.

As she turned, a man emerged from the shadows. At first she assumed he was an employee of the hospital, but he abruptly grabbed her and hauled her up against his chest, wrapping his arms so tightly around her she could barely breathe.

"Help!" she screamed, but her voice was weak, and the man roughly clamped a hand over her face. When he dragged her backward, panic surged.

No! This couldn't happen! *Help me, please!* Shauna struggled against her assailant, using her elbows and her feet to lash out against him. But he was strong, built like the dark-haired man who'd stabbed Leah, and he effortlessly dragged her the short distance to what she realized must be a service road, where a long, dark sedan was waiting.

He forcefully thrust her into the car so recklessly she smacked her head on the edge of the car roof, at the same spot where she had several stitches from the car crash. Her *kapp* slipped off, and pain zinged through her head. She tried to ignore the discomfort as the sedan lurched forward, moving down the road.

How had they found her? Had they been following her the whole time?

"Who are you?" she gasped, turning to face her attacker. He was built like a tank, but it wasn't the dark-haired man who stabbed Leah. This guy had shaved his head bald and had narrow, beady eyes.

"My name isn't important," he said with a sneer.

"Then where are we going?"

"To meet my boss."

"Who is your boss?" She belatedly realized the bald guy was wearing a cop uniform. It was black in color, like the ones Liam and his deputies wore, but it looked different. It took a moment for her to realize there was an emblem on his sleeve for the Chicago Police Department.

Liam and Garrett had been right about law enforcement being involved. She wasn't sure how a cop from Chicago had gotten the information he had, but it was clear he and the driver of the sedan had known to look for her at the hospital after the dark-haired guy had been shot.

Baldy smirked. "First, the boss wants to make sure we have the right woman this time. Then you'll learn the rest."

She stared at him, trying to figure out what he was talking about. Right woman? Because they'd goofed up with Leah? She glanced at the driver, who was ignoring her. She still felt as if this was related to her biological father. But, of course, this guy wasn't willing to fill in the gaps.

The names in her mother's diary popped into her mind.

"I'm assuming the man who hired you is either Warren or Douglas," she said, hoping to surprise him enough that he'd keep talking.

"Close, but no," Baldy said. The evil smile on his face made her realize how much he was enjoying this.

"Someone close to Warren or Douglas, then." She shrugged. "I guess it doesn't matter. But you should know the sheriff won't stop until he finds me."

Baldy didn't answer. It occurred to her that maybe they had been on the wrong track. That the person who'd hired these guys, and the others, too, wasn't her biological father.

It rankled that the man sitting beside her was a cop.

Wasn't he supposed to uphold the law? To put criminals behind bars?

Not kidnap innocent women.

She told herself to stay strong, but as they left the hospital behind, she was hit with an overwhelming wave of despair.

Liam would never find her. Not until it was too late.

Not until after they'd killed her.

Liam shifted his weight from one foot to the other. Something was terribly wrong. Shauna had disappeared, and he felt certain it wasn't of her own volition. He called Garrett and asked for additional deputy support to search the hospital property.

Deep down, he felt as if he'd failed Shauna. The same way he'd failed Jerica and Mikey.

Especially Mikey.

Spinning on his heel, he returned to Leah's room, the last place anyone had seen Shauna. When his gaze landed on the stairwell, he moved toward it. Maybe she'd taken the stairs instead of the elevator? He'd noticed that she'd looked uncomfortable at the various people who'd stared at her in her Amish clothing.

The stairs led down to the ground level and straight outside. He stood for a moment on the sidewalk, trying to imagine what Shauna might have done if she'd come this way. Gone for a walk? It seemed unlikely, but he felt compelled to check anyway.

He followed the sidewalk around the side of the building. After a few yards, he frowned when something white at the side of a service road caught his eye.

He rushed forward, his stomach dropping to the soles of his feet when he recognized it as an Amish *kapp*.

It must be the one Shauna had been wearing.

He knelt and picked it up along the edge, placing it in an evidence bag. Rising to his feet, he fought off the feeling of helplessness.

How long ago had she been taken? Not long, but without anything to go on, he had no idea where to start searching for her. His phone rang, and he grabbed it. "Harland."

"Liam, I have something on the Ford truck, license plate starting with the letter *A*," Garrett said. "I'm on my way to the hospital, but I knew you'd want to know. The truck is owned by a guy named George Kinner, and here's the best part—Kinner works for Warren Richfield."

"Warren Richfield." It took a moment for the name to register. "You mean Illinois governor Warren Richfield?"

"Yeah. A man who has a lot to lose if the news that he fathered a child with a sixteen-year-old stripper came to light. It makes sense that he wouldn't necessarily care about any legal consequences, since he can claim ignorance on Shauna's mother's age, but the political fallout would be detrimental. He'd never win another election, that's for sure."

It was a clue, and a good one. "Great work, but Shauna has been taken by whoever Richfield has hired. We need to find her, Garrett."

"We will," Garrett assured him. "Hang tough. I'll be there soon."

Not soon enough, Liam thought as he pocketed his

phone and jogged back to the hospital. He went back inside and headed straight for the information desk. Flashing his badge, he said, "Green Lake County sheriff Liam Harland. I need to view hospital security tapes ASAP. A woman has been abducted and I need to find her!"

The woman behind the desk blanched. "I'll call Security."

"You do that." He drummed his fingers on the counter with impatience. Hospitals were considered private property, and as such, they didn't have to share their video without a court order. When the head of Security arrived, a man by the name of Alex Smith, he looked hesitant when Liam voiced his request.

"Maybe I should call my vice president."

"You can do that, but you need to understand a woman's life is in jeopardy and time is of the essence. Please, I wouldn't ask if this wasn't important."

The guy wavered, then caved. "Okay, let's see what we have."

"Thank you. I appreciate your cooperation. There's a side exit she took that leads to a service road." He stared at Smith. "Please tell me you have cameras in that area."

"We have tons of cameras," Smith said, taking a seat behind a large console with six computer screens. "I know the area you're describing." He tapped several keys and soon brought up the one that Liam needed.

"There! That's her!" He touched Shauna's figure with his fingertip.

"She's Amish?" Smith asked.

"Yes." Liam didn't want to waste time explaining. "I found her *kapp* on the ground at the street."

"Okay, let me zoom in a bit." Smith hit more keys, and they watched in silence as Shauna walked outside and lifted her head up to the sky. She continued along the path, clearly lost in thought, when they saw a large man come out from the shadows.

"Freeze that image," Liam ordered. "Magnify his face for me."

Smith did as he asked, and Liam grimly stared at the bald man who'd grabbed Shauna. He didn't recognize her assailant, but when he saw the uniform, he knew his original instincts had been correct.

The guy was a cop. Not one of his, thankfully. He knew every one of his deputies personally.

"That's good. I'll need you to print a copy of his face," Liam said. When that was done, the printer nearby whirring as it spit out the image, he gestured to the screen. "Now keep the tape running. I need to see where he takes her." Liam silently prayed the cop hadn't killed her and left her hidden in some alcove somewhere.

"He really assaulted her," Smith said, his eyes wide as he did as Liam requested. Clearly the security department didn't often have felony crimes happening on their property.

Liam watched grimly as the bald man dragged Shauna to a black sedan. Shauna struggled, fighting to free herself, but to no avail. The bald cop shoved her into the back seat of the vehicle. Liam winced when she hit her head against the edge of the car, and he saw that was the moment her *kapp* had slipped off. The cop didn't seem to care about the injury or her *kapp*, because he crowded into the back seat beside Shauna, pushing her farther inside. The moment he closed the car door, the driver took off.

It was horrifying to watch the entire sequence play out. "I need a license plate number," Liam told Smith. Then he called Garrett. "Cancel the deputies responding to the hospital. I have video showing Shauna was abducted. They shoved her into a black sedan and left."

"I'll call them off, but do you have more for us to go on?" Garrett asked.

Liam turned to grab the photo that had come off the printer. He snapped a picture with his phone and quickly texted it to Garrett. "This is the guy who took her. We're still working on the vehicle information."

"Got it. Call me when you have more," Garrett said.

"Thanks."

Smith worked the keyboard for a few minutes. "From the side view, we can only get three numbers, five-eight-two. But when I try to get the full plate from another angle, it's blurry."

He battled a wave of frustration. Three numbers were better than none, since he'd noticed the car was a black Lincoln sedan, but he needed more.

He desperately needed to find Shauna.

"Print that partial license plate photo for me, too," Liam said.

"Okay." The printer whirred again. "Looks like that same sedan is heading west on the highway." Smith tapped some keys and activated another camera. The video showed the sedan gliding away from the hospital campus. Smith glanced up at him. "Any chance they're heading back to Green Lake?"

"Maybe." Why they'd go back to Green Lake, he wasn't sure. "Will you please bring up the image of that bald guy again? I need to make out that insignia on his uniform."

Smith obliged and blew up the image. It was just clear enough for him to read *Chicago Police Department*. The way the cop was holding Shauna against him prevented him from seeing a name tag, if he was wearing one at all.

Not likely when committing a crime.

"I need copies of this video sent to my email address." Liam rattled it off as Smith jotted it down. "I'm taking this photo with me, too."

"Understood." Smith tapped more keys. "Video is on its way, but keep in mind, it may take a while to load. Our internet access can be bogged down at times."

Waiting for the video to load was akin to watching paint dry, but it didn't take as long as he'd feared. The moment it finished, he grabbed the second photo off the printer, turned and headed outside to his car.

He called Garrett. "I'm texting you a picture of the partial plate on the sedan. The bald guy who abducted Shauna is a Chicago cop. They were last seen in a black Lincoln sedan, partial plate number five-eight-two. Get a BOLO out for them right away."

"Consider it done, boss. Where are you going?" Garrett asked.

Liam threw the squad car in gear and hit the red lights and siren as he barreled out of the parking lot. "I'm going to try to catch up with them."

"Roger that."

Liam knew his chances of catching up with the Lincoln were slim to none. But he had to try. He hoped the driver of the sedan would stay within the speed limit rather than risk being pulled over for speeding.

But there were also several highways they could take to return to Green Lake. If that was even where they were going. He chose the main highway, hoping they'd taken the direct route rather than risk winding around less traveled highways, but really, he had no idea where their final destination was.

It could be anywhere. Here within Green Lake County, or anywhere in the entire state of Wisconsin.

Even all the way down to Illinois.

No. The moment that thought entered his mind, he swiftly discarded it. They wouldn't risk taking Shauna all the way back to Illinois. Not when her mother had been murdered there and her apartment had been set on fire. Her body being found there would raise too many questions.

Besides, it was a long drive—several hours if they stayed within the speed limit. And that would provide too many ways for them to be found, especially once they crossed the state line and went through the Illinois tollway. Tollways kept electronic records and took pictures of license plates.

That wouldn't be smart, and these guys had eluded capture thus far. His gut was telling him they'd stick around Green Lake. That was where they'd left their other murder victims, Jeff Clancy and Karl Maxwell. Both of those victims had been left in the same spot, but he didn't believe they'd go three for three.

No, they'd find another place. But where? There was a lot of area to cover with a limited number of deputies. Even if he pulled in the help of the state police, they were working at a distinct disadvantage.

There were far too many acres of land with various hiding places to stash one woman.

One potentially dead woman.

Don't go there, he warned. He couldn't concentrate on the task before him if he thought the worst. He needed to believe Shauna was still alive.

He lifted his heart and silently prayed for God's guidance and wisdom.

He had to find Shauna—he just had to!

Liam couldn't bear the burden of another failure.

FIFTEEN

Shauna gave up fighting against her captor, hoping to conserve her strength. If there was an opportunity to get away, she planned to take it.

Better to die trying to escape than to be handed over to her executioner.

He'd checked her for a phone, his hands rough. It was all she could do not to swing at him. Instead, she kept a keen eye on their surroundings, just in case she was able to make a run for it.

"I don't know why you can't explain where we're going. It's not as if I can tell anyone." She glared at Baldy and tried to reach the door handle behind her. It would be a big risk to open the door and attempt to get out when they were traveling at fifty-five miles per hour. But when they slowed down? Then she could make her move. "Why the big secret?"

"Shut up," Baldy snapped. "And don't bother trying to get out of the car. The doors are locked." He smirked again. "Gotta love those child safety rules, don't you?"

He could be bluffing, but she sensed he wasn't. Still, she kept her hand on the handle, just in case he was lying. "Fine, don't tell me. But it looks as if you're heading back to Green Lake."

The statement was a bluff of her own, since one set of wooded highways interspersed with acres of farmland looked exactly like the other, in her eyes. But then she saw a glimpse of a highway sign announcing Green Lake was ten miles ahead.

Was it a good sign they were taking her back to Green Lake? She imagined meeting Baldy's boss and tried not to shiver.

"Slow down, Eli. We can't get stopped for speeding," Baldy growled in a low tone.

The driver muttered something under his breath, but the car slowed down. She filed the driver's name away for future reference. If she had a future.

Which wasn't looking likely.

Her heart hammered against her ribs, and she struggled to remain calm. What would happen when they reached their destination? The boss would look her over and decide she was Shauna McKay, his biological daughter? And then what? He'd pull out a gun and kill her?

She shivered. As horrible as it sounded, she couldn't imagine a scenario where she survived this kidnapping.

There must be some way to escape. But how?

"Bill, there's a red flashing light behind us. It's pretty far back, but do you think it's the cops?"

Baldy, aka Bill, turned and swore. "Yeah, get off the highway now! And do it without hitting your brakes. At this distance, the cop can't identify our vehicle."

Liam! Shauna was convinced Liam was behind

them, but her elation was short-lived. Eli abruptly turned off the highway at the next intersection, then hit the gas hard. The sedan leaped forward, the tires eating up the pavement.

Please, Lord, show Liam the way!

There was a tense silence in the sedan. Eli turned at the next intersection and gestured at Bill. "Which way? I don't know how to get there from here."

Get where? Shauna wondered.

"Hang on. I have the GPS on my phone." From her position pressed up against the door, she couldn't see Bill's screen. "Stay on this road for another five miles."

Shauna peeked over her shoulder, dismayed to see nothing but empty highway behind them.

Don't lose hope. God is watching over me, and Liam won't rest until I'm found.

Hopefully alive rather than dead.

As they continued along the road, though, she knew it would be impossible for Liam to have followed them. Too many rural highways with too many potential places to turn off.

Especially since Liam had no idea where they were going. The location where the so-called boss was waiting for her.

The sedan slowed at the next intersection, most of them uncontrolled by stop signs. In a desperate move, she pulled the door handle and pressed against the door.

It didn't open.

"I told you it was locked." Bill the bald man smirked again. Then he held up a beefy fist, shaking it in front

of her face. "Try that again and I'll knock you uncon-
scious."

Swallowing hard, she shrank from him. Oddly
enough, she'd rather face whatever waited for her
head-on with both eyes open than be rendered un-
conscious and unaware of what was happening.

Even if that meant watching as the boss killed her.

"Take a left up ahead," Bill said. "Then we go two
more miles and the property is on the right."

What property? She wished she'd paid more attention when Liam had driven her from one place to the
next. One thing was for sure—she did not recognize
this stretch of highway. It was more rural, and they
hadn't passed a single car since taking it.

But when Eli turned left, she straightened in her
seat. Now, this spot did look familiar. Was that Davy's
house in the distance? If so, why on earth would Eli
and Bill bring her here? She didn't for one minute believe Davy was involved. He could have hurt her long
before now.

Feeling Bill's gaze on her, she frowned, pretending
not to know where they were. When she saw another
vehicle parked along the side of the road, the knot in
her stomach tightened.

No doubt, the boss was inside the second sedan,
waiting for her to be handed over like a slab of meat.

But to her surprise, the black sedan followed them
up the long driveway of Davy's house. The windows of
Davy's house were dark, and she assumed that meant
the place was empty. Her uncle didn't have electricity, but when they'd gone inside for the boxes, she had

seen several lanterns. The same kind Elizabeth had used at her house.

She was relieved Davy wasn't home.

Then a horrible thought hit. Had they already swung by the Amish Shoppe to grab Davy, too? Had they brought him here? Was it possible he was tied up inside?

"We're here," Bill said in a weird singsong voice. She intensely disliked him—not only was he a disgrace to the uniform he wore, but he was a horrible human being.

A man who enjoyed taunting others, seeing them afraid and in pain.

She ignored him, refusing to play his sick game. When the sedan stopped, Eli waited for several moments for the occupants of the other car to emerge and hurry inside Davy's house. Now a lantern came on, casting an eerie glow. As if that was some sort of signal, Eli slid out from behind the wheel, then opened her door.

Bald Bill crowded right behind her, making it impossible to make a run for it. As she emerged from the sedan, Eli roughly grabbed her arm. Bill took the other one. And together they half dragged her all the way to Davy's house, entering the building through the back door.

As she'd feared, Davy was there, tied to one of the chairs he'd made by hand. There was a gag over his mouth, and his apologetic gaze met hers.

"Let him go!" She tried to pull out of Bill and Eli's grip, but they were too strong. "My uncle isn't involved in this!"

"Silence," Bill said, tightening his grip on her arm to the point she feared he'd crush her bone to pulp.

Shauna tried not to give in to the wave of despair. Even if she could get away, making a run for it, she couldn't leave Davy behind.

"Get her over to the light so I can see her face." A sharp female voice caught her off guard. The woman was standing in the shadows, far enough away that Shauna couldn't see her face clearly.

Eli and Bill dragged her closer to the light. The glare made it more difficult to see the woman who she deduced must be the boss.

"That's her," the woman said in a voice that dripped with disdain. "I can tell by her facial features she carries his blood. The Amish disguise is good, I'll grant you that, but she's no better than her stripper mother." She let out a hard laugh. "Your mother should have known better than to try to blackmail us. We don't pay up—we get even."

Who was this woman? She couldn't see her face, but Shauna put on a brave front anyway, managing to find her voice. "Really? A simple look is all it takes for you to kill me and my uncle? Shouldn't you get a DNA test to confirm your husband is my biological father? Or don't you care how many innocent people you've hurt and killed?"

The woman stepped forward. Shauna could see her features clearly now, and her familiar face made her gasp. No, it couldn't be.

But it was. The first name Warren should have been a huge clue. The woman standing in front of her was Helen Greer Richfield. The first lady of Illinois.

Governor Warren Richfield's wife.

This was the reason her mother had been murdered.

Somehow her mother had figured out Richfield was Shauna's biological father. And she'd tried to black-mail them with the information. The solution? Kill her mother, to prevent the scandalous news of Shauna's birth father impregnating a young girl from coming to light. Nothing more than simple greed and a desperate need to keep the illusion of the perfect political family alive.

Despite their rotten core.

And in that moment, she knew this woman, who stared at her with cold, hard eyes, didn't care about anything but keeping her current position at the governor's mansion.

Helen Greer Richfield would kill her and Davy without batting an eye.

Liam had noticed the car way up ahead of him on the highway turn off, which had made him suspicious it was the sedan he'd wanted. He'd pushed the squad car as fast as it could go but had still lost them.

Panic clawed up his throat, but he tried to think logically. If that car had been the kidnappers turning off the highway, they'd brought Shauna back to Green Lake for a reason. When his phone rang, he hit the hands-free button. "Talk to me, Garrett."

"Listen, I've done some research on Warren Richfield," Garrett said. "Sounds like he has a tight election race coming up next year. And get this—he was giving a speech outside at a local football stadium a month ago when a drone malfunctioned and hit him on the forehead."

"Why does that matter?" Liam asked.

"The press made a big deal out of the fact that he has some genetic clotting disorder, one that causes his blood to clot faster than normal. It made me wonder if that was what might have caught Shauna's mother's attention. Maybe Shauna has the same clotting disorder."

The memory of his meeting Shauna the first time flashed into his mind. She'd hit her head on the steering wheel, but by the time he'd reached her side, the wound had already stopped bleeding.

"She does," he said. "I'm sure of it. We need to find that sedan, Garrett, and soon."

"Every deputy is on alert," Garrett assured him. "If that vehicle is on the road, we'll find it."

And if it wasn't on the road? Liam swallowed hard. "Any property in the area owned by Richfield?"

"None that I've found," Garrett said. "Not unless he's put the property under another name."

"Maybe check his wife's maiden name," Liam suggested. "We need something, anything to go on."

"Okay, hang on a minute." Liam heard Garrett working the keyboard. "His wife is Helen Greer Richfield. Her father's name is Albert Greer, and she has a cousin, Roland Asher." More silence, then a sigh. "I don't see anything listed in Green Lake County under any of those names."

"Try the counties nearby," Liam urged.

"Okay, but that will take some time. I'll call you if I find something."

"Thanks. Oh, and stay close to the radio, in case I find the sedan."

"Roger that," Garrett agreed.

The news of the clotting disorder swirled in his

mind. Was it possible that Warren Richfield had come all the way here to Green Lake? He and his wife didn't have any property that they'd been able to find, so where would they go?

An abandoned house? There were many possibilities there. But how would Richfield know where to find them?

David's house?

He frowned. It seemed risky for them to take Shauna there. Yet the gunman had been there the other night. Maybe they suspected Shauna's mother had evidence of some kind? Like the diary? He wasn't sure a diary would hold up in court, but then again, if Warren Richfield's goal was to avoid scandal, Linda McKay's diary would be key. And she might have even told Warren she had proof.

Maybe that proof was the reason Shauna's apartment had been set on fire.

He tightened his grip on the steering wheel. This rural highway wasn't that far from David's place.

While it wasn't logical they'd take Shauna there, he couldn't afford to ignore the possibility. Especially since he didn't have a destination in mind.

He quickly cued up Garrett on the radio. "Listen, I'm going to swing by David's house. It's probably vacant, but I want to rule it out as a possible location."

"Understood," Garrett said. "I'm at headquarters, but call if you need backup."

"I will." Liam shut down the red lights and siren, opting for stealth. As he'd been traveling in the opposite direction, he turned around and headed toward David's place. The longer he drove, the more he felt as if he might be on the right track. The lack of logic didn't dissuade him. The property was far enough out of town and away from other homes to be a good hiding spot.

When he saw the dim light in the distance, his heart began to pound. He told himself it was possible Davy had brought Elizabeth there for safekeeping. The Amish Shoppe would be closed by now. Still, he couldn't deny the strong sense of urgency.

A mile from David's house, he abruptly hit the brake and pulled off along the side of the road. The light was enough to raise his suspicions, and there was no point in alerting whoever was inside that he was there.

At least, not until he knew what was going on.

He slid from the vehicle, pulling his gun from its holster. Dusk had fallen fast, and this far out, there wasn't a lot of ambient light. Still, he stayed low as he lightly ran along the side of the road. There weren't enough trees to keep him hidden, but he used the ones that were there as best he could.

Several minutes went by before he was able to see the area around David's house more clearly. The single light coming from one of the living room windows was dim. It made sense, as he knew David used battery-powered or gas lanterns for light.

He crouched near a small tree about twenty yards from the property. Then frowned as he saw the outline of a long black sedan.

Not just one of them, but two of them, almost identical in size and shape.

This was it! Liam knew God had brought him to the very location where the kidnappers had brought

Shauna. Yet the sight wasn't reassuring. Why were there two cars?

Did that mean Davy was a prisoner, too?

He was reaching for his radio when he heard another car engine coming along the road behind him. He dropped down, flattening himself against the earth to avoid being seen. To his surprise, the vehicle, a small red truck, pulled into David's driveway and rolled to a stop right behind the other sedan.

What in the world?

He crawled along the ground using his elbows and knees to get closer, not daring to use his radio. In the silence of the night, he heard the truck door slam. From his position he couldn't see the driver but imagined that person heading inside to join the party.

Liam continued crawling across the damp grass for a few minutes, then risked getting on his feet. He lightly ran the rest of the way to the house, glad that there didn't seem to be anyone guarding the place from the outside.

He wanted to know what they were dealing with, particularly how many perps were inside, before he called Garrett for backup.

The back door to David's house wasn't all the way closed. Shimmying between the vehicles, being careful not to touch them lest he set off any alarms, he crept closer, straining to listen.

He didn't hear anything. Remembering the layout of David's house, he knew the back door led into the kitchen, while the living area was located beyond that. Reaching up, he tried the door.

It opened without making a sound.

Weapon ready, he eased inside, then abruptly stopped

when he saw a man standing near the doorway leading from the kitchen into the living room. Thankfully, his attention was riveted on the occupants in the living room, so he hadn't noticed Liam.

The driver of the red truck? He thought so, as it was clear the newcomer was listening intently to the conversation going on in the living room.

"I'm telling you, there's no reason to kill us." Hearing Shauna's voice was like a punch to the gut. "I don't want anything from you other than to be left alone."

"Why did your mother try to blackmail us?" The female voice made Liam frown. He'd expected Warren Richfield, although it could be that the governor was here, too. Hence the two sedans. "It's too late, anyway. Things have gone too far. Your stupid mother has left me no choice but to get rid of you once and for all."

"Why kill me? It was your jerk of a husband who got my mother pregnant in the first place. It's not my fault he's my father." Shauna's voice was taunting, and Liam could just imagine the fury on Helen Greer Richfield's face.

"Wait a minute." The man who'd been hiding near the doorway abruptly stepped forward. "Is it true? Is this woman my half sister?"

"Kevin, what are you doing here?"

The implication of what was happening clicked into place. Kevin was Warren and Helen's son.

"Ever hear of GPS tracking, Mom?" Kevin asked impatiently. "I knew you were up to something. You've been so secretive lately, so I followed you. Only to find out I have a half sister!"

"Nice to meet you, Kevin," Shauna said. "How old are you, anyway? I'll be twenty-four in January."

There was a moment of silence before Kevin stepped forward. "I'll be twenty-four in February." The young man spun to stare at his mother. "Please tell me you didn't know about her all this time."

"You need to leave, Kevin, right now!" There was a hint of hysteria in Helen Greer's tone. "You can't be anywhere near this mess, understand? You can't be a part of this!"

"A part of what? Killing my sister?" Kevin let out a harsh laugh. "I always knew you and Dad didn't love each other as much as you loved money and power, but this? You're honestly going to kill my half sister and whoever that guy is you have tied to the chair to keep them quiet? Murder? Come on—that's outrageous, even for you!"

The tension in the room ratcheted up several notches, and Liam knew time was running out.

Waiting for backup to arrive wasn't an option. Unfortunately, there was only one of him, and from what he could see, at least two other men, maybe more in the room. All likely armed.

It didn't matter. He'd have to make a move, sooner than later.

Before the entire situation spiraled even further out of control.

SIXTEEN

"Please, there's no need to do this." Shauna did her best to calm things down despite how she was reeling on the inside.

It was one thing to learn the circumstances around her mother's relationship with her biological father, but seeing her half brother standing a few feet away was incomprehensible.

They were the same age. Born a month apart. Shauna felt bad for Helen Greer Richfield, and she could only imagine how devastating it had been for her to learn of her husband's infidelity. Especially if her mother had confessed he'd fathered a child that was close to her own son's age.

Not to mention, learning he'd cheated with a much younger woman. A sixteen-year-old stripper.

"Kevin, I'm not going to tell you again. Get out of here!" Helen gave her son such a withering stare that if the situation was reversed, Shauna imagined she'd have done exactly as she'd been told.

Kevin didn't.

It gave her an appreciation for her mother. Despite

her mother's failings, there had been no doubt that Linda had loved her.

This woman didn't seem capable of loving anyone.

"Or what?" Kevin challenged. "You're gonna shoot me, too?"

"Don't be ridiculous," his mother snapped. "Don't you see I'm trying to protect you? I need you to be far away when we take care of things here."

Take care of things was a strange way to describe cold-blooded murder. One thing was for sure—her brother's unexpected arrival had thrown a wrench into Helen's plans. If not for Kevin, she was certain she and Davy would already be dead.

She glanced at Davy, trying to come up with a plan to use Kevin's presence in mounting an escape. Davy's calm gaze didn't show any fear, and he nodded his head, giving her permission to do whatever was necessary.

But what?

Movement from behind Kevin caught her eye. She tried not to stare in that direction so no one else would notice. Risking another quick glance toward the spot, she knew someone was standing there.

Another bad guy? Or Liam?

A bad guy would likely jump forward to grab Kevin, forcing her brother out of the house and far away from here. No, her gut told her the lurker must be Liam. How he'd found her here was a mystery, but she was grateful to know she and Davy weren't alone.

Outnumbered? Yes. But not alone.

Before she could come up with a plan, Liam jumped

forward, grabbed Kevin and pulled him out of the way. "Police! Drop your weapons, now!" he ordered.

Helen Greer Richfield turned to stare at Liam, then at where her son was standing behind him. "Don't listen to him." She glared at Eli, Bill and a third man who must have been in the car with Helen. In a heartbeat, Bill stepped forward and put his gun against Davy's temple.

Shauna sucked in a quick breath. "My uncle isn't involved in this!"

"Drop your weapons," Liam repeated sternly. He reached out and snagged Kevin's arm, drawing her brother closer to him. "We can exchange hostages, or you can risk losing your son, Mrs. Richfield. Your choice."

"You wouldn't dare," she hissed. "Do you know who I am? You're a small-town sheriff. I'll make sure you never get another job as long as you live."

"You're a murderer and I'm not letting you get away with such a heinous crime," Liam countered. "Choose!"

The way Helen Greer Richfield wavered made Shauna feel bad for Kevin. To have a mother like that, one who only valued money, prestige and power, must have been awful.

"Gee, thanks, Mom. Glad to know how high I rank in your life," Kevin said harshly. Then he surprised everyone by ripping away from Liam and lunging toward his mother, his fingers clawing at her face.

Shauna didn't hesitate. She abruptly turned toward Davy and Bill. The bald cop had stepped forward as if to protect his boss from Kevin's wild attack. When

Shauna realized he no longer held his gun on Davy, she rushed Bill, hitting his solid girth with both hands as hard as she could. He was a big man, but she put all her weight behind the thrust.

With surprise on her side, Bill stumbled beneath the force of her blow, hitting the edge of Davy's living room sofa with his knee. Davy threw himself sideways in his chair, toppling into the third unknown man, knocking him off balance. Chaos ensued, Helen screaming as Kevin pummeled her. Liam had gone after Eli, quickly disarming him.

"No!" Bill shouted, lifting his gun toward Liam.

"Stop!" Shauna rushed him again, determined to save Liam's life. Bill turned toward her, but the sound of a loud kick, followed by the front door of Davy's house slamming open, made him pause.

It was all she needed. Fueled by anger and resentment at how her mother and Jeff Clancy had been murdered, she locked her fingers around Bill's gun hand and pushed with all her might upward just as the gun discharged. The shot was incredibly loud, and a bullet punctured Davy's ceiling. Drywall dust rained down on them.

"Police! Put your weapons down, now!" Garrett and another deputy rushed inside as two other deputies came in through the back door.

Liam held Eli as Garrett helped disarm Bill. Another deputy rushed forward to grab the third man. The two deputies who'd come in through the kitchen managed to pry Kevin and Helen Greer Richfield apart.

Shauna was shocked at the scratches Kevin had left on his mother's face, but the woman didn't seem to notice. As the deputy handcuffed her wrists, she seemed to lose what little rational thought she had left.

"Let me go! You can't do this! Do you know who I am? I'm the first lady of Illinois! You must release me right now! I demand a lawyer!" Her face was an ugly mottled red, and once again, Shauna almost felt sorry for her.

Almost.

The deputies placed Eli, Bill, Helen, the third man and Kevin in custody. Helen continued to rant even as the deputy attempted to inform her of her rights.

Finally, he clapped a hand over her mouth. "Ma'am, you have the right to remain silent," he repeated. "I suggest you exercise that right. You'll get an attorney, but not until we've booked you for kidnapping, murder and attempted murder." He removed his hand, and she stared at him, then glanced at her son.

"This is your fault," she said bitterly. "If you hadn't come here…"

"Give it a rest, Mom," Kevin said wearily. "Nothing is ever your fault or Dad's fault, is it? All this time I thought you were smart, but you've proved to be dumber than a common criminal."

Shauna couldn't help feeling proud of her half brother for stepping up for what was right. And while she would have never asked him to attack his own mother, she had to admit Kevin had provided the distraction they needed to get control of the situation.

Belatedly remembering Davy, she knelt beside him. He was still tied to the chair, lying awkwardly on his side. She quickly removed the gag from her uncle's mouth, then worked at the binds. Her hands were shaking so badly, she couldn't get traction on the knots. Liam came over with a pocketknife and quickly cut through them.

"Are you okay?" Liam helped Davy to his feet, then turned toward her. "Shauna? Are you hurt?"

"I'm f-fine." She entwined her fingers to stop them from shaking. "How on earth did you find us?"

"I had a hunch about this location and got here in time to see Kevin go inside." Liam gestured toward Garrett. "The real question is how the rest of the cavalry arrived. I didn't have the chance to call for backup."

"Elizabeth came to the police station in a horse and buggy driven by one of the Amish elders, right after we spoke, Liam," Garrett said. He smiled at her uncle. "She was worried about you, David. Said you would never have left her alone at the Amish Shoppe and was convinced something had happened to you. Without a phone or another way to notify us, she came in person to alert us to your kidnapping."

"They caught me off guard," Davy admitted. "Especially the one dressed as a police officer. But I didn't fight lest I draw attention to Elizabeth." He smiled gently. "I wasn't afraid to die. I've made peace with God. I was more worried about Elizabeth and Shauna."

"The cop doesn't deserve to wear the uniform." Liam scowled. "And I plan to make sure the only uniform he wears from this point on is an orange prison jumpsuit."

"Bald Bill," she said. "I only know their first names. Eli was the driver, but Bald Bill is the one who grabbed me outside the hospital. The third guy must have come with Helen Richfield."

"His name is Roland Asher. He's Helen's cousin," Garrett said. "I found his picture online."

"We saw the entire abduction on the hospital security video," Liam said. He reached out to touch her arm, then drew her into his embrace. "I couldn't believe it when you rushed him, Shauna. He was armed. I was worried sick he would shoot you!"

"He didn't, and I didn't care if he did." She lifted her head to smile up at him. "Honestly, Liam, I just wanted to stop him from hurting you or Davy." She glanced at her uncle. "Your calmness helped me, too. I knew you were thinking about God's plan for us, and that gave me the strength and courage to act. And the way you managed to take out the third guy, Roland Asher, was brilliant, too."

"I'm glad, Shauna." Davy smiled. "Linda would be so proud of the woman you've become."

Thinking about her mother reminded her of Kevin. She reluctantly pulled out of Liam's arms to turn toward her half brother. It was disconcerting to realize he was staring at her.

Talk about a strange way to meet a brother she hadn't known she had. She felt awful for him, especially since he looked just as shocked by the way the events had unfolded.

"Kevin provided the perfect distraction. I couldn't let it go to waste. Especially since I didn't know there were other deputies nearby." She paused, then added, "Liam, why has Kevin been arrested? He hasn't done anything wrong."

"He physically attacked his mother," Liam pointed out. "But I can chalk that up to extreme emotional disturbance. I won't press charges against him. The poor kid has had enough trouble in his life—no need to add to it."

The kid was only one month younger than her. She gripped Liam's arm. "Will you take his handcuffs off? Please? I—I'd like to talk to him."

Liam hesitated, then reluctantly nodded. They went over to where Kevin stood next to one of the deputies. "Remove the restraints. He's a witness, not a perp."

"Okay." The deputy did as he was told. Both the deputy and Liam took a few steps back, leaving her and Kevin a modicum of privacy.

"I—owe you a debt of thanks," Shauna said. "You saved my life, and my uncle's life, too."

"Yeah, well, I can't say I'm happy to meet you, but I couldn't just watch you get murdered, either," Kevin said. He shook his head. "This is all so messed up. I knew my mom had been acting strangely, but this? Planning a double homicide? That's over-the-top, even for her."

"I know. And I'm sorry." Shauna stared up at him. "I wish there was something I could do to help, but I'm as much a victim in this as you are. I am here for you, though, if you need me."

"Yeah, thanks, but I think I'll pass. Can't say I'm happy to learn my dad cheated on my mom." A flash of uncertainty shadowed his gaze. "And I'm sorry, too. My mother—well, I don't know what to say. Her actions tonight revealed a side of her I didn't know existed."

"Desperation can cloud a person's judgment." It was the most diplomatic thing she could think of to

say. "I'll be honest—it won't be easy for me to forgive what she's done. My mother and my friend were
murdered just so she could keep her position as the
governor's wife."

Kevin looked away, as if he couldn't bear to relive
the gory details. She understood.

A wave of exhaustion hit hard. The nightmare was
over, and for the first time since receiving that fateful phone call from her mother, Shauna knew she was
safe.

Lives had been ruined, though, including hers.
Nothing would ever be the same.

She watched as Liam moved through the house,
taking charge of the crime scene. Her heart squeezed
painfully in her chest as she realized her time with him
was over. As hard as it would be, she'd have to return
to Chicago, to piece together what was left of her life.

But she would miss Liam. He'd protected her, kissed
her, captured her heart and made her want the type of
life she'd never imagined having. A family he wasn't
looking for—at least, not anymore. Understandable,
considering he'd lost his wife and son on the very night
he'd learned she was leaving him.

Somehow, Shauna would have to find a way to live
without him.

Liam fell back into his role as cop, although his
gaze constantly drifted back to Shauna.

The moment she'd gone after Bald Bill, he'd known
how much he loved her. He'd rather place his own life
on the line than risk hers. Today and always.

He wanted to tell her. To hold her close and to kiss

her, but they were hardly alone here. Not to mention, she had a lot to deal with right now. Bad enough the governor's wife had tried to have her killed, but learning about her half brother must have been equally unsettling. Maybe more so, as he was another innocent victim in this.

In his mind, it was a strange turn of events that Kevin had inadvertently helped save her life.

Liam stepped back for a moment as the deputies took over taking photographs and collecting evidence. It hit him like a tidal wave that God had brought him through difficult times, gut-wrenching losses, so that he would be right here, tonight.

"You feel God's peace, too, don't you?" David came up to stand beside him.

"Yes." It was as simple and complicated as that. "I believe God has been watching over us all along. That everything happened for a reason."

"Yes, it has." David's smile faded. "I will miss my sister, but I believe she's in a better place now."

Liam nodded, thinking the same about Jerica and Mikey.

"Have you told Shauna how much you love her?"

David's question hit him out of the blue. "How do you know that?"

"It's in your eyes when you look at her." David lifted a brow. "It's much the way she looks at you, too."

"I don't think so," he began, but David gripped his arm.

"I do. Trust God's plan, Liam. Don't let this opportunity get away."

His gaze returned to Shauna, the way a magnet

finds bits of metal, and he slowly nodded. Shauna didn't trust men in general after the way her boyfriend had lied to her, but maybe he could convince her to give them a chance. "I'll drive you both back to my place for tonight. We can decide what to do next come morning."

"That's a good plan, but I would like to stop by Elizabeth's house to let her know I'm okay."

"Absolutely." Liam knew that if not for Elizabeth, they wouldn't have been able to control the gunmen so easily. If Garrett and the other deputies hadn't arrived when they did, he was certain more blood would have been shed here tonight.

His, Shauna's and David's. It was a humbling realization.

"Shauna, will you allow me to drive you and David back to my place?" He hoped she wouldn't balk. "We can decide next steps in the morning."

"Sure." She looked exhausted. "Why not?"

"Wait here. I left my car down the road." He gestured for Garrett to follow him outside. "I need to get Shauna and Davy out of here. Can you handle things here?"

"No problem. We'll take care of documenting the crime scene." Garrett slapped him on the shoulder. "You did good finding them, boss. If you hadn't, we might have arrived too late."

"I know, and I owe Elizabeth, too, for sounding the alarm." Liam jogged down the road to his squad car. Then he headed back to the house just as Shauna and David emerged.

He ushered them into the car. Davy sat in the back,

and Shauna slipped in beside him. She was unusually quiet, probably still reeling from the recent events.

"Where are we going?" She frowned as he turned toward the Amish community.

"David wants Elizabeth to know you're both safe," he explained.

"Of course." Shauna lifted a hand to her bare head. Her dark hair had mostly fallen from her bun, framing her face. "I hope she's not upset that I lost her *kapp*."

"She won't be," Liam assured her. "We can replace it, or better yet, I'll buy one of her quilts."

Shauna nodded. "I will probably need one, too, since all my stuff has been lost in the fire. It will wipe out my savings to replace everything."

Liam's stomach knotted with tension. She was planning to go back to Chicago?

He waited for her to elaborate, but she didn't. He pulled up in front of Elizabeth's house. His cousin opened the door before David managed to get out of the squad.

"Praise God, you're not hurt, David." Elizabeth clasped her hands together.

"Thanks to you, Elizabeth," David said. He lightly touched her hand. "Shauna and I are both fine. The danger is over, and I owe you a debt of gratitude for the way you helped protect my niece."

"'Twas no hardship, David. I'm just grateful you are both unharmed."

The two stared at each other for a long moment before Elizabeth stepped back. "I must go. *Mammi* Ruth is waiting."

"Good night." David inclined his head and waited until Elizabeth had closed the door.

Liam knew the two had feelings for each other, but Elizabeth had lost a husband, and David was not a member of the Amish community. And even then, he could tell there was something more holding them back.

He looked over at Shauna, who had clearly noticed the underlying emotion between them, too.

"It's an impossible situation for them, isn't it?" she asked as David slowly returned to the car.

"Nothing is impossible, Shauna. Not if you want it badly enough to fight for it."

No one spoke as he navigated the highways to his place. He led the way inside, then gently grasped Shauna's arm. "Can we talk?"

"Ah, sure." She dropped into a kitchen chair. David continued through the house, disappearing into the bathroom.

"Shauna, I need to tell you something." He moved his chair closer so that they were directly across from each other.

"I'll pay you back…" she began, but he shook his head and lifted a hand.

"No, please, that's not it. Shauna, I've fallen in love with you. I hadn't planned on it. In fact, I tried hard not to let you get too close. Mostly because I was afraid of being hurt the way Jerica gutted me when she decided to leave me to return to Madison."

"Oh, Liam, I know that must have been so difficult…"

"It was, but not anymore. I mean, I'll always mourn them, especially my son, but tonight I realized that

God has given me a second chance, Shauna. God brought you into my life, and into my heart."

Her eyes widened. "Are you sure? I mean, we've barely known each other a few days."

"I'm absolutely sure. I know you don't trust easily, but I promise I've never lied to you." Her reaction wasn't exactly what he'd been hoping for. "And please know, I won't rush you into anything. You can take all the time you need."

A smile tugged at the corner of her mouth. "I thought I was rushing things," she said wryly. "Because you need to know, I love you, too, Liam. Having a family wasn't anything I'd dared hope for. Not after the way my previous boyfriend lied to me. Not to mention the way my mom and I struggled to survive. I figured I was better off alone, but now?" She lifted her hand and cupped his cheek. Her gaze clung to his. "God has shown me the way, and I realized tonight that my life is meaningless without you."

"Really?" Hope bloomed in his heart, and he covered her hand with his. "You're not just saying that to appease me?"

That made her laugh. "Oh, Liam, you should know that I would never tell a man I love him just to appease him."

He chuckled. "I do know that. I admired your bold survival instincts from the first moment we met." He stood and drew her up so that he could pull her into his arms. "I love you, Shauna. And I know you have to go back to Chicago to straighten things out, but I hope you'll come back to Green Lake. Or, if you can't imagine living here in the middle of nowhere, I'll move to Chicago. Garrett will make a great sheriff, and I'm sure I can find another job as a police officer."

"It's sweet of you to offer to move, Liam, but Davy is here." She smiled up at him. "I've learned the importance of family, too. I rather like the idea of living here."

"Family is important, and it starts with us—you and me." Liam lowered his head and kissed her, knowing in his heart that God had brought them together to save them.

And so that they could save each other.

EPILOGUE

Shauna borrowed Liam's SUV and spent three weeks in Chicago taking care of everything she'd abruptly left behind. She met with the insurance agent on her burned apartment and her totaled car, cleaned out and sold her mother's trailer, and arranged for her mother's body to be sent to Green Lake for a proper burial.

All necessary things, but while she spoke to Liam frequently, she missed him more than she thought possible.

More than she'd ever missed anyone.

She closed her bank account and put the few belongings she'd taken from her mother's trailer and the clothes she'd purchased in the back of the SUV. Then she made the trip back to Green Lake.

Surprisingly, the closer she got to the town, the lighter she felt. As if she were shedding the darkness of her past and starting anew. And maybe she was.

Helen Greer Richfield, Eli Kern, William "Bald Bill" Donahue and Roland Asher had all been transferred from Green Lake to Chicago to face charges of first-degree homicide in the killing of her mother and

Jeff Clancy, not to mention the other guys who'd been helping them. The last she'd heard, Eli was spilling his guts, telling everything he knew to get a lighter sentence.

Shauna had been warned about the possible need to testify at Helen's trial, but she wasn't worried. Rumor had it that Warren had already filed for divorce, claiming he had no knowledge of any criminal activity his wife was involved with. He'd also resigned his position as governor, effective immediately, a direct result of the scandal. Ironic that Helen's actions had brought about the very thing she'd tried so hard to avoid.

The loss of living at the governor's mansion.

She hadn't heard from Kevin, her half brother, but she hadn't really expected to. Maybe one day he'd reach out to her. She prayed for him every night.

Along with Davy, and Elizabeth, and of course the man who held her heart.

Liam.

When she was ten miles out of town, she called him on her new phone. "Hey, I should be at Davy's in ten minutes or so." The plan was that she would stay with her uncle, without electricity or running water, until she could find an apartment of her own.

"I'm already here," Liam said with a chuckle. "Can't wait to see you."

"Me, too." She ended the call, unable to wipe the sappy smile off her face.

She pulled into Davy's driveway, parking behind the squad car she knew had been driven by Liam, since she'd borrowed his personal SUV. Liam strode out of the house to greet her and pulled her into a tight hug.

"I missed you," he murmured against her hair.

"Ditto," she managed before he kissed her.

Wrapping her arms around his neck, she returned his kiss, knowing this was where she belonged.

Liam finally broke off the kiss, then dropped to his knee. He looked up at her, a wide grin on his face. "Shauna Margaret McKay, will you please do me the honor of becoming my wife?"

"Oh, Liam, is this just because you missed me?" she asked, hardly able to believe he was really proposing.

"You don't know me very well if you think I'd buy an engagement ring and propose just because I missed you," he teased, throwing her earlier words back at her. Then his expression turned serious. "I asked David for permission to marry you, and he agreed. So it's up to you now, Shauna. Will you please marry me?"

"Yes." Then she laughed and repeated, "Yes! I'd be honored to be your wife."

"I promise to put my family first," Liam said somberly. "Always. And I won't lie to you, ever."

"Me, too," she agreed. "Because marriage takes two people, Liam. We both need to work at it to succeed."

He smiled, stood and pulled her close. "I'm so thankful God brought us together."

"Me, too, Liam." She hugged him tight. "Me, too."

* * * * *

Dear Reader,

Thanks for reading *Hiding in Plain Sight*, my first Amish suspense! I hope you enjoyed Shauna and Liam's story. I visited the Amish community here in Wisconsin and was so impressed with their faith, community and craftsmanship I knew I needed to write this book. I hope you'll be happy to hear I'm working on Elizabeth and David's story next.

I adore hearing from my readers. Without you, I wouldn't have any reason to write. I can be found on Facebook at www.facebook.com/LauraScottBooks, on Twitter at twitter.com/laurascottbooks, on Instagram at www.instagram.com/laurascottbooks and through my website at www.laurascottbooks.com. You may want to consider signing up for my monthly newsletter, too. Not only will you find out when my new books are available (like Elizabeth and David's story), but I also offer an exclusive novella to all subscribers, which is not available for sale on any venue.

Until next time,
Laura Scott

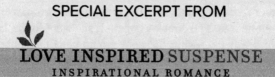
Even before the shouting and the woman's scream, Laura Devin sensed that something was wrong in the lobby of First Federal Bank. The bright morning conversation between bank employees stopped abruptly, but it was what she saw on her computer screen that told her they were in the middle of a bank robbery. All the alarms and cameras had been disabled, just like with the other small-town banks that had been robbed in the last two years.

Her back was to the open door in the room next to the lobby, where she was working at a computer. When she whirled her chair around, she could only see the back of one of the tellers. Then she saw a flash of movement on the other side of the counter.

"This is a bank robbery! Do as I say, and no one will die here today!"

Even if one of the tellers had time to push the silent alarm, it had been disabled. The police would not show up.

Laura's gaze jolted to her purse across the room, where her phone was. The door was open. If she went for it, they might see her. Closing the door would alert the robbers to her presence that much faster. But she had no choice.

She sprinted across the carpet and grabbed her phone, pressing 911.

"Hey, there's somebody in that room! Get her!"

The operator came on the line. "What is your emergency?"

"Bank robbery—"

A hand went over her mouth. She dropped the phone before the thief could grab it from her. He must have seen that she was making a call, or at least heard the phone when it landed on the carpet. And yet, he didn't tell her to pick it up. Maybe it was still on and the operator could hear what was happening.

He whispered in her ear, the fabric of the ski mask he wore brushing over her cheek. "It's going to be okay. Just do what they say."

Don't miss
Christmas Hostage *by Sharon Dunn.*
Available wherever Love Inspired Suspense books and ebooks are sold.

LoveInspired.com

LISEXP0822